WATCHA GONNA DO BOY...

WATCHA GONNA BE?

WATCHA GONNA DO BOY...

WATCHA GONNA BE?

Peter Taylor

Fitzhenry & Whiteside

Published in Canada by Fitzhenry & Whiteside,
195 Allstate Parkway, Markham, Ontario L3R 4T8

Published in the United States by Fitzhenry & Whiteside,
311 Washington Street, Brighton, Massachusetts 02135

www.fitzhenry.ca   godwit@fitzhenry.ca

10 9 8 7 6 5 4 3 2 1

Library and Archives Canada Cataloguing in Publication
Watcha Gonna Do Boy...Watcha Gonna Be?
ISBN 978-1-55455-323-5 (Paperback)
Data available on file

Publisher Cataloging-in-Publication Data (U.S.)
Watcha Gonna Do Boy...Watcha Gonna Be?
ISBN 978-1-55455-323-5 (Paperback)
Data available on file

Fitzhenry & Whiteside acknowledges with thanks the
Canada Council for the Arts, and the Ontario Arts Council
for their support of our publishing program. We acknowledge
the financial support of the Government of Canada through
the Canada Book Fund (CBF) for our publishing activities.

Cover design by Daniel Choi
Text design by Tanya Montini
Cover image by iStockphoto

CONTENTS

PART I

1//   MEMORY I: You're finished school but don't stop now boy: WATCHA GONNA DO BOY ... WATCHA GONNA BE? The handshakes, kisses, slaps on back, the cards and socks and ties and rings, and WATCHA GONNA DO BOY ... WATCHA GONNA BE? Those twelve fun years are over now. You've got to make your mind up soon. Might do you good to work a year, or are you heading off to school?

Eh?

WATCHA GONNA DO BOY ... WATCHA GONNA BE?

He's seventeen and proud as hell, and so are they, and so is everyone. The baby's finished school and all growed up; and Papa beams, and Mama cries, and look at him, and look at all of them. You gonna work or on to school? WATCHA GONNA DO BOY ... WATCHA GONNA BE?

Well fuck, I think I'll work a year! I'll join the railroad, yes I will. I'll work a year. Should do me good. A lot of fellas do you know. I'll work a year and grow up some, and then I'll go away to school.

And four months later here he is.

I'm flat broke now, and sitting on my bunk car bed, and staring at this telegram:

GRANDAD PARALYZED STOP STROKE STOP DOCTOR SAYS WILL NEVER WALK AGAIN STOP CAN YOU GET HOME?

And Ray Malone is singing at the old tin sink and splashing underneath his hairy arms with aftershave and scrubbing at his yellow teeth and spitting out the bunk car door.

I musta read it forty times.

At eight o'clock, I follow him across the track and

down a mud path to the bar. HOTEL BELAIRE HOTEL BELAIRE HOTEL. The neon sign. Not raining yet, but feels like rain. That train comes through at ten o'clock. I'll catch it in to Edmundston and take a bus. I'll just have two quick beers, then go.

But I think I might as well have three.

As a matter of fact, I'll have me four.

And now I might as well have five cause I'm singing at the bar with Ray Malone.

I like the way these Friday nights go by.

They shut the jukebox off when Ray walks in. "YOU ODDA GEDDA BANJO TOO": he's telling me. "YOU'D NEVER HAFTA BUYA BEER." And someone gives us two more free.

Faces staring, laughing, shining, singing out the English words they know. It's nine o'clock in Rivière Bleu, Quebec, and Ray keeps singing song on song, and we keep getting beer on beer; I'm flying now and singing loud's I can with Ray. No club car on that train to Edmundston. So I can sleep. We're singing "Mountain Dew," "Redwing," "Frank and Johnnie" (Ray's own song, which doesn't quite get through French ears); "Good Night, Irene," for some old girl who's just bought us another beer. I'm flying now.

And Ray gets tired standing up and sits us at a table talking, talking for himself and me. I don't talk French. He gotta tell them everything I say.

TWO BEER!

And then the jukebox starts to hum. The plugs and clugs of quarters light it up, and two young girls who look like sisters, maybe twins, are dancing with each other on the floor. Ray sees this first and drags me on the floor to dance with him. This jammed-up floor and everybody's kidding Ray and coming to our table just to laugh with him. We sit back down.

MY GOD, you'd love the women here. Black-eyed and hard in tight black dresses, sweaters; walking, strong on big thick child-bearing hips and thighs and calves and big French feet. French and heavy-titted in their high-high heels.

TWO BEER!

I'm in the can and CHRIST it's ten o'clock! I gotta go! It's raining and I'm running and I know the train is gone. That train don't even stop if no one's there. Goddamn the luck!

There's no one at the station now. It's open, but even the clerk is gone. There's nothing left to do but laugh, and it strikes me funny in a hopeless way and I sit down drunk, then leaning on a urinal, I sing Ray's song:

O Frank and Johnny were lovers,
O Lordy How they could love,
Frank kissed John at the station
While the big moon shone above …
He WAS his man
But he was doinit wrong.

Then back outside it's raining harder now, and muddy all around the station house, but I don't fall, and pretty soon I'm back inside that big hotel and singing again, right next to Ray, who didn't even notice I was gone. So now I'll have to catch the morning train.

TWO BEER!

I'm dancing with some woman now and getting close to talking French. I do when I get drunk enough. She's big and happy. Dressed to kill. It's Friday Night! The jukebox playing rock 'n roll lights up the corner of the room. A hundred couples dancing now; she wants to jive!

I'm flying now and show a little footwork just for Ray, who's laughing at me from his chair. And soon we're bumping heads and hips and shoving people everywhere. Big heavy girl with thighs as big around as me. I twirl her and she disappears into the crowd. Damn Ray sees this and doubles up, and tells some guy in French what I've just done.

TWO BEER!

Then sitting down again and GOD I'm drunk, and get to talking French at last with some young girl who's sitting here and just CAN'T be here all alone:

"*Quel âge avez-vous?*"

"*Quinze.*"

"QUINZE!"

"*Oui.*"

"*Où est votre garçon?*"

She giggles at my French and claps her hands in time to music from the giant jukebox. I ask again if some guy's here with her:

"Are you alone? Where are your friends?"

She points around the room to everyone.

"*Tout le monde!*"

I laugh at her. Then down to work and using every goddamn word I know.

"A walk? You? Me? Go for walk? *Promenade?*"

With all my teeth, my finest smile. And no one at the table seems to see or care.

She smiles and rubs her leg on mine. I guide her hand.

"Okay?"

"Okay."

Outside I have to hug her hard. Make sure she's real or some damn thing. And doing this I stumble, trip, but stay up, arms around her tight, and then, around the corner, kiss her mouth. And kiss her mouth again, again. It's big and wet for just fifteen.

I'm dizzy when my eyes are shut. I gotta stop. And no talk now. Not even French. I head her for the bunk cars down the track and kid-around and kiss her on the face again. She's hot, so tuck my fingers in her bum.

NO! Gotta tell Old Ray I'm gone. Don't want him walking in on me.

"You wait right here. You understand? I have to see my friend, okay? I go see Ray, okay?"

"Okay."

QUINZE!

Goddamnit Ray, now where'd you go? The banjo, where's that damn tin thing?

He's gone!

He can't be gone.

He's gone!

So in the can for one quick piss. Can't leak along the path

or track. Might scare her off. And worry that she might be gone. But there she is and takes my hand, and up along the path we go and kiss her head. The mud-path's wet, but no more rain, and up we go—me worried all the time she's gonna ask me where, but keep on walking, getting soaked, our feet and legs.

It's not too far to the bunk cars now.

And here's the track and down the track the bunk cars sided in the dark. We stumble on the hard wet ties. She trips. I trip. We laugh a lot, and I try walking on the rail. Her high heels, one in each hot hand, are useless now. She carries them and off we go.

The key! The key! The key is gone, but ooops! The door's not even locked. So up I go and take her shoes and sit them on the floor inside, then tug her up the ladder to the door. And hug her, feel her, back her up toward the bunk and SMASH! CLANG TWANG!

That Goddamn banjo!

"SSSSHHHHHHHHHHHHHHHHH."

And whispering: "That you Malone?"

"Yeah SSSHHHHHHHHHH."

Whispering: "I'll take the other car, okay?"

"Okay."

And she is QUINZE from head to feet and throwing clothes around the place and wanting even more than I. All oooooing aaaaahing, ooooooooing scratching now. Hot legs around me, bouncing on that railroad bunk, and IN and out and IN and out and IN and out and IN and out, like some small piston on a model train; the only man's job boys do well, and just half dizzy in that dark old car I shoot her in the stomach of her fire box and feel my body straining into hers. It's all black now. I melt into her skinny arms and then to sleep.

I never dream on nights like this.

2// The screaming was what woke me up. And standing yelling at my bunk is some wild woman grabbing me and kicking me with big bare feet. She's yelling French and punching me, but can't get loose from Ray Malone. He's holding her as best he can. They're both half-dressed. It's like a goddamn dream but hurts too much. My head is aching like it's gonna crack, but she doesn't care.

I can't get up or out of bed. Got nothing on. And there's my girl, my little girl. She's yelling, crying, pulling on her skirt.

I'm half asleep, but no one seems to give a damn. My little girl is yelling now. Her sobs have stopped. At last I hear an English word. My little girl. I hardly hear it in the fight, but there it is:

"MAMA MAMA MAMA … MAMAAAA!"

GOOD GOD!

3//
                                        Rivière Bleu, Que.

                                        September 2, 1959

Dear Mom and Dad:

A terrible thing has happened. It seems like only yesterday Grandad was well. When your telegram arrived I was shocked. I am making arrangements to get me home as soon as possible, but it could take two or three days. I hope everything will be okay until then.

Things like this are enough to make anyone think about dedicating his life to science or medicine. I hope Grandma is well. She will take it hard.

Just last night I was telling Ray Malone (you've heard me speak of him often) what had happened. If it is of any comfort, his father had a similar stroke several years ago, and today he is as healthy as ever.

Will be home in a couple of days. As fast as I can get there.

                                        Your Son,

                                        Peter

4// MEMORY II: Peter William — —, age five sitting on the front-porch steps of your trackside home in New Brunswick, or maybe down a little closer to the track, up on a fence (still in your own yard), and waving to your Grandad Hero who would give a blast on his engine whistle that was just for you. A whistle TOOT, and a heavy wave of his big gloved hand that always dropped you from the fence, or brought you to your feet up on the steps where, one big smile on spindly legs, you'd imitate his wave and stand there breathless, counting boxcars as they clack-clacked by your eyes. Sometimes he'd drive a passenger, and there you'd stand, your head flicking— flicking to the click of wheels along the track, and you'd stand there waving, waving to everybody on that goddamned train.

And you'd wonder how many people, especially kids your own age, knew who was driving that train.

But you missed the real rail-rolling railway. I mean the only one you ever knew, the only real one, was the one he worked. And from stories that you heard him tell and crazy little night-and-day-dream visions that you had, you built your own, then sat all day along the track pretending you were there … *Maritime* … *Ocean Liner* … *Bay Train* … *Scotian* … just names today. Not sounds to warm a pot of tea, or set a clock … like when the whole damned thing was railroad.

And when you got there the smoke was gone, the steam was gone, the coal was gone, the grease was gone, and the fire was gone, and the railroad was losing its railroad.

And everywhere were clean young men in clean lean grey-and-white striped greaseless, creaseless coveralls with shiny tin lunch cans, capless, and looking like so many factory workers. Gone was the grease and coal dust from the pockets and bib of those many-miled, hung-in-the-kitchen work clothes, the boxcar jampacked lunchpail of beautiful grey sheet metal and the beat up cap. They were even taking the jog from under the wheels with ribbon rail, and the lonely night-time wail of hot-rod freight trains had been traded for a cheap electric horn.

NATIONAL RAILWAYS
Application TR32-740

Name :   *Peter William* ■■■■■

Address :   *29 ½ Edward Avenue*
                         Campbellton, New Brunswick

Date of Birth: *June 20, 1942*

Sex: Male   Married: *(~~Yes~~) (No)*

Education: *Queen Elizabeth High School,*
                         Campbellton, N.B.
                         Graduated XII A, June 1959

Physical Disabilities: *(~~Yes~~) (No)*:
                         If Yes, please list in the space
                         provided: *None*

NATIONAL RAILWAYS   **TR32-740**   **(2)**

Previous Employment: *(This will be my first job)*
(Please do not list summer employment):

Military Service: *No*

This space to be completed by examiner:
I recommend that Peter William ■■■■■ be hired as a signalman's helper for the NR Signal Department at Moncton, N.B.

Date: *June 20, 1959*

Signature: *Peter* ■■■■■

PART 2.

6//   Sitting in the shade of a boxcar, ass on track on the mainline side and rolling smokes, one, two, three, and sticking them in my workshirt pocket for a walk up town where the people are. That's me! Mind on nothing but tobacco papers and how in hell you work them. I never rolled before, but here I am anyway, sporting my first pair of boots, a khaki shirt, stiff blue starchy dungarees, and these goddamn makings.

"WATCHA GONNA BE, A RAILROADER A COWBOY?" my kid sister yelled when I got dressed.

Just sitting here and looking down the track till sun goes down. Tomorrow we move out I hear, to open up another ditch ten miles away. Been here two days.

Amherst, N.S.

June 27, 1959

Dear Mom and Dad:

Well here I am all settled in and tired too. The work is hard. The days are long. You were right, a year at this will do me much good. The job is fun, but a good example of what a lack of education can lead to. The majority of men here have not finished high school, and dig ditches to prove it.

I am officially billed as a signalman's helper, imagine that! This means I dig trenches, bury cable, and climb poles to string telegraph wire. They offer several courses in basic electricity here which promise, more or less, to add a little money to your pay cheque. I have started one. They think I have chosen my career, and I say what they don't know won't hurt them. All the money I can save will go toward my first year of university. If these first two days are any indication, I don't know if I'll last a year! HA HA!

One old timer here, the cook, knows Grandad. He worked with him on the I.N.R. At nights after I have finished reading the electrical manuals, I slip into the cook car and chat with him about the old-time railroad. He's a pretty fine fellow. Say hello to Grandad for him, and for me. His name is Sam, and he comes from Saint John. I missed his last name when he introduced himself and don't like to ask him now.

Did you notice the postmark? I was sent on to Amherst as soon as I reported for duty in Moncton. So here I am in Nova Scotia for the first time.

Once again, I think it was a wise move on our part, and I will certainly look forward to going on to university next year.

Well I must turn in as tomorrow is a long, hard day.

Best wishes,
Peter

8// Behind me, rooted to the track, the cook car looses water to the greasy ties and creaks as sock foot, Sam the Cook completes his day. Old Sam and me. Old lazy after-supper night. Old railroad town.

> **9//** Your life-long dream of being there was two days old; and those two mornings swinging pick beside the track (nine railroadmen with you), when truckers honked their diesel horns and waved their rolled-up shirtsleeve arms, when schoolkids stopped to watch the trains roll by, and townfolk stopped a while to watch you

work; you thought you'd never live enough to live it down.

GOD, you were with them, looking at yourself through love-shot eyes, and couldn't keep yourself down on the track. From every car gone by you'd wonder who the YOUNG GUY was; in every schoolboy's eye you saw yourself as THAT'S THE KIND OF MAN I WANT TO BE; ; and as a townsman, THERE'S A FINE YOUNG BOY.

10// GOD, I was RAILROAD through and through and wouldn't have it any other way. I'd sometimes shave, more often not, then all decked out at eight o'clock, away I'd go, my dirty dungarees and shirt. I wouldn't even scrape my boots, all caked with mud. A RAILROADMAN, and off to town where the people are with everything but a goddamn lunchcan.

11// The guys on that first gang were older'n me. Sam the Cook, and Barry Wells (I don't remember Sam's last name), and BIG DAN DEWAR foreman there who I saw one day hoist a motor car onto the track like it was a toy (eight hundred pounds). Big Dan could pick more ditch than two good men could shovel. And he didn't like you late for work. Then Normand Proulx and Hank LeClerc who kidded me'n my scrawny arms. And Gus Mahoney, Frank D'Amour, and Eddy Roy. Another guy the gang called Moose seemed all the railroadman I hoped to be; hard-working, lean, and strong as hell. Hard playing too, and loud; though later I met Ray Malone.

Big curly burly Ray Malone with yellow teeth and dirty hair. In Edmundston at 2:00 AM (didn't really meet him then, but saw him coming in that day, all boozed and tired, through the bunk car door). Arrived in Edmundston that day myself and found the cars and found my bunk, and thinking all that Sam had said could hardly wait to meet this guy. I walked around. There's no one here.

Ray's gang, but Ray's gone.

It's midnight, so I climb in bed.

And I hardly got to sleep that night, a Friday night, but thought about Mad Ray instead. I wondered what he looked like, where he was, and read a book. My bunk was down the wall from his, with mine up top and his below (seniority on railroad gangs). His denim coat was hanging there. His boots, a battered cap, a dirty towel, were scattered all around his bunk. And hanging on the wall beside his bunk, all chipped, but strung, the banjo I would hear him play.

"Can't play the thing, but needs it for to sing," Sam said. And there it was.

I fell asleep a dozen times, but woke again. His bunk was

empty, no trains due. Just like the stories Sam had told. Old Ray in Truro, Moncton, too, and one wild tale of Halifax. He'd disappeared a week that time. He's gone again, I told myself. He'll have the foreman on his back for sure; remembering what Sam had said, how weekends he'd just up and go.

I should have gone to sleep right then, but something Sam had said said no.

HE TAKES THAT BANJO EVERYWHERE HE GOES!

He can't be far, I tell myself, then fall asleep. But woke up soon when SLAM the bunkcar door fell shut. Then SLAM again. He stumbled to his bunkside, yawned, yanked off his sweater, looked around, and yawned again.

It's Ray Malone.

I feel like screaming, "I'M AWAKE" or "WELCOME HOME" or some fool thing. I would today. But new here now and no one knows me yet so I just watch.

Old Ray is only thirty-two and still the guys all called him Old, or Mad or Crazy Ray. "Though Raymond is my really name," I heard him joke so many times. Old Ray since he was just a kid. Not looking like I thought he would, but no one could; not all that big, about my height, a few grey hairs you'd notice in the morning sun, small dark brown eyes, and eyebrows like two flops of fur. Got bunchy shoulders from the track and big rough arms, and black and curly, dirty hair.

He stood beside his bunk awhile, then sat and pulled his Hart shoes off. "Good shoe for walkin," told me once, and laughed when I went out and bought a pair: "You like my style!"

It must be 2:00 AM, but I can't sleep.

Next morning, shaving in a bowl, I watched him climbing from his bunk, then nodding over half-fried eggs. And last man on the track, not just that day but every day he'd hop up on that chugging motor car and shout, "LET'S GO," like he was boss. Then on the track, he worked like hell, his pick or shovel chopping, digging, like a wild machine. I'd watch him for a while, then fall in just as close as I could and grunt and groan the way I do.

"He'll sleep at noon," a voice who sees me watching says. And sure enough when noon hour comes and hungry men sit down to eat, old Ray curls up in moss and shade, just off the track, and sweats and snores and shoos off flies.

HO HUM, it's time to work again, and just like morning, Ray's the last one there; though soon catching up so no one could say he didn't earn a fair pay cheque. Got loafers on this gang like any gang, but Ray's not one.

Mid afternoon we bury cable, tamp the ground, then stand and wait while foreman Eddie Linden checks his list. The cables in, the boxes wired, potheads, bootlegs, keys in place; then paces off more yards along the track and stops to make more notes on pad.

"Sam says hello," I get a chance to say at last. He smiles, big wide yellow grin, and drops his ass down on the rail. "He told me I should look you up when I got here. I saw you coming in last night." And keep on talking while he wipes his neck.

"HOW'S SAM?" he says, and I say, "FINE," and find myself talking loud because he always does. And then he talks and I sit still. "He'll talk your head off," Sam'd said.

And away he goes: "KEERIST I usedta drink when I knew Sam and poor old Sammy never took a drink as you know well and usedta say to me GODDAMNIT RAY YER GONNA KILL YERSELF but I was crazier'n hell back then and never paid no never mind though evertime he picked me up I'd tell him SAMMY I'MA GONNA QUIT but he'd just laugh and slop me with water from the drinking pail and tell me I was just a young feller and that havin fun the way I was doin was just parta growin up. YERA FINE WORKER RAY he'd tell me don't let the booze getya down. KEERIST WHEN I THINK OF IT. How is he anyway?"

And: "HEY he ever tell you bout the time we swiped the motor car and drove from Rivière Bleu to Edmundston? Not Sam and me but a whole bang of fellas from old George McGregor's gang? Dodgin trains all the goddamn way then left it on the track while all of us ran in for beer. SMASH! THE WHOLE THING GONE TA HELL. Coulda been fired but there was too many of us envolved."

O GOD! He talked like that.

12// And back on that first gang again. That's Sammy's gang …

And here the bunkcars (three of them) would bring the local cops around to shouts and curses, singing, whooping, drinking beer; but as the cops would say to Sam: "It's better here than up in town!" Then maybe 2:00 AM, Old Sam'd yell to GET TO SLEEP and things'd settle down okay. Not foreman Dan, but Sam the cook, whose job would have him out of bed while they snored on.

You never stopped to think about old Sam. Old Sam was there. And yet my fondest memories of that small gang are Sam. Small things, like his first day's "You'll like it here," and, "Where ya frum boy?" I still hear these from time to time. And Sam's GEDDOUDDABED for three long weeks. Big Old Fat Sam. The dishpan hands and slippered feet looked wrong somehow on such a man.

And CHRIST that day in Amherst, on the track at 10:00 AM when I arrived and found him sitting in his sun-lit kitchen door and he said: "BILLY BATEMAN'S YOUR GRANDAD! WELL I'LL BE

DAMNED" I thought I'd die. Old Sam had worked with Billy years before, when Bill was driving work trains on the I.N.R.

And I told Sam, and Sam told me, a dozen stories about the man.

13// When news of Grandad's stroke caught up with me in Rivière Bleu, I thought about Big Sam again. And running down the track that morning, tripping on the ties and scared as hell, I got to wishing Sam was there, cause Sam would know just what to do. He'd tell me how to act when I got home. He'd likely seen a hundred strokes before. At least he coulda told me how he'd look. Grandad I mean. And that's what seemed to hurt me most. It's hard to picture Grandad paralyzed.

AND HOW IN HELL WAS I TO KNOW SHE'S JUST FIFTEEN?

In any case I caught that train and sat there crazy shaking, sweating, thinking any minute cops would come through dragging that poor little girl; and thinking how she'd walk up, standing by my seat, and pointing, talking to the cops, and all in French, while helpless there I'd be without a thing to say. Got thinking how they'd gather evidence (you read about it all the time) … the hair! That goddamn hair routine, and ran into the bathroom in my car and ran my comb all through my pubic hair. The fingernails! I cleaned those too. Then washed my cock, all soft with fright.

But luck was with me, train pulled out on time, and nowhere was a sign of cops, or little girl, or old Mama.

Goodbye Rivière Bleu. Goodbye Little Girl.

I sat back in my seat and tried to sleep.

14// With the guys on that first gang much older'n me, I'd go out alone most nights, and walk up town and stroll around, and feeling tough the first time in my life in those strange clothes, I'd belt black coffees in the greasy spoons and wink at whores along the street. Not whores by trade like Montreal, but women wanting money bad for cigarettes and beer; just plain old women any man could buy.

So I'd walk by and wink at them.

15// —I think I'd better work a year, you told your Dad.

—You have a job?

—I hear the railroad's hiring … it's signal work … the training's good.

—You'll go to university next year?

—I will. I promise you. And he agreed.

So packed your bags and boyhood railroad dreams, and there you were.

16// And soon along the track all day the guys would ride me … NIGHTMAN … TAILMAN … WHOYA GONNA DO TONIGHT … and I was feeling big as hell. We're moving up and down the Nova Scotia track, from Amherst into Truro, and the work is tough.

17// NOVA SCOTIA: Small railroad towns I call all these, cause that's the way I remember them (though not because my own home town was any more), where never more than two, three blocks I'd stroll around the station part of town where tall and shingled, brown and grey, the town-old homes of town-old families stood silent in the early night, and trackside peoples of the railroad world all set their clocks to the sound of trains and ate their stew and baked bean meals with hot black tea.

18// THE WOMAN I WAS WINKING AT WORE RUNDOWN SHOES: I read that somewhere, years ago. Now she kept coming back to me, and every time I went around a corner I'd find her standing there and winking back. One block she'd wear a bright but faded dress with one-time sash. The next she'd wear an open coat, but my young eyes, despite my feeling tough as hell, would stop at the lapel, or in a wink. Four feet away and walking fast, I'd catch the smell of perfume bought downtown, or booze, the smell of which I didn't know. And always those damn rundown shoes.

I'd note the corner street sign well and next day tell a breakfast tale or two (say where and when and how and who) to start the day. And sometimes even Sam'd laugh, though all the time he's betting on the whore. The little man for Sam was dressed in silk. Big Businessman in $100 vest walks by, and Sam'd mutter: There's the reason people's poor!

And then that night in Truro, a woman, maybe forty, winked at me and took me home.

Old ten-buck bill was all I had when I walked in. Old railroad clothes'n a silly grin when I came out.

OLD WOMAN, I'LL REMEMBER YOU.

19// Then home to bed. But just before I got back to the cars, or to my own, I hopped up on a flatcar sided there, and dreamed an hour on my back.

The corset gone, her hips and thighs were more than soft. Her belly bulged.

Her answer to my over-eager hands just: "Not for $10," and left her sweater on, her skirt hiked up around her hips.

Her answer to my over-eager self: "You through?" Then dressed and back out on the street again, all knowing now, and satisfied. Imagine that!

And telling it at breakfast that next day when Sam just

laughed: "You crazy fool."

Then noon hour I began to itch.

20//   OLD WOMAN, I'LL REMEMBER YOU.

21//   We moved to Folly Lake next day where for two hot days we dug up year-old cable, put down new, and dug in potheads at the joints between the rails, and planted keys here while a work gang lifted track.

Muscle and bone, these criminal-looking work gangs, with now and then an ordinary guy who'd look so strange that even Moose'd whisper: Hell's he doin here?

And Sam treated me for crabs.

22//   Amherst, N.S.

                                        July 10, 1959

Dear Mom and Dad:

It's been several weeks. Hope you are all well. Was very happy to get your letter and read up on the news back home. It gets a little tiring reading nothing but electrical manuals, etc.

You are right about the Canada Savings Bonds; they are probably the best, easiest, and safest way to save money. I have asked our foreman Dan Dewar to pick me up the necessary forms. I have opened a savings account at the Amherst Branch of the Bank of Nova Scotia, and it is starting to look good. I call it my University Fund.

Met a lady in a bookstore here just yesterday who said her son had worked a year before going to university and she said he is doing very very well. Writing some papers here next week for a small certificate in electrical maintenance. Nothing much, but it might add a few dollars to my salary. Have been thinking lately I might very well go into electrical engineering. I find the work here can be quite interesting and electricity, as you probably know, is certainly an exciting field.

Bye for now,
Peter

23// Was quite a thrill for me by then, the walking down the street at night five-hundred miles from my hometown and feeling like I'd never had a care. A working, laughing, rolling railroadman. I like it and it's plain to see I'm happy here. You know the feeling: lived at home most all your life, two bucks a week for movies and a date, the creeping in on even Friday night at 12:01, and everyone in town knows who you are. Was mad about it right away and started staying out most every night. And often taking off on weekends for Moncton to see my former hometown buddy Jim Solomon.

When I go back to the cars at night, there's no one on the street at all. The towns look empty but for one or two small lights somewhere. And not a sound except my own sore feet.

24// MEMORY III: It's the sound of being grown up. The no-more sound of creeping up the stairs at night. Jalopy where the bike once stood, and all that jazz. You try to see it all at once. You never can. Remembering at once the smell of schools, a holiday, and giant forests in your own backyard. Two bushes and a stump for jungle war. Two lilac bushes and an apple tree for a big game hunt. A thousand favourite dreams gone small. The speaking now to giants you tongue-tied watched while they with unbelievable skill repaired a car or built a fence.

And everything was railroad then. You didn't stop to look around. You ate it, drank it, sucked it up. RAILROAD. And like a new-found girl-friend then, it was all too beautiful for you to see. The days went by, the weeks went by, and Nova Scotia never looked the same or ever will.

25// I'm happy then and earning money like I've never seen before. The guy who held the interview said engineers come from the ranks, and what would Mom and Dad say then? He said I'd make it if I stuck it out.

> **26//** So dropping all the memories of home, the promises to everyone, with big-shot letters just to keep the peace, you fell in railroad right up to your ears. The big AT LAST … A DREAM'S COME TRUE … I'M HERE … I'M ON THE RAILROAD … Don't look back.

27// And working like I never worked before, and trying hard to catch the boss's eye; but he doesn't care. And I realize, working's hard as I can, I'm only doing one man's job. And eating like I never ate before, and eating some times just to catch Sam's eye; but he doesn't care. And I realize, eating all I can, I'm only eating one man's meal. I'm working, laughing, having me a time. And digging ditches, miles of ditches, eighteen inches deep and one foot wide, in mud or rock with aching arms and blistered hands, and happy. Seventeen years old!

The guys here playing poker all night long, or off up town and getting drunk to stumble in here after twelve and WHOOP it up. And I'm off almost every night, except when sitting in with Sam who's quite a bit like Grandad. He talks the same and laughs the same. And Sam's a cook, and Bill's an engineer. A railroadman's a railroadman.

28// And Nova Scotia, 1959: there's railroad towns and countryside and friendly people everywhere you go. In Amherst, Truro, Folly Lake ... in little-sized towns and middle-sized towns, the trains don't leave coal dust at all. The railroad cuts across and through like a railroad should. It's summer and I'm fresh away from home. A railroad signalman!

29// You had a pass they gave you for the job to—say, if you were transferred—get you there, and warned you not to overdo the weekend trips to home. The whole damn gang took it home each week. But being quite a trip to my hometown, and being, too, so fresh away, I never went. Instead I'd hang around the station part of town, or in the cars, or walk for miles along the track, talking to people everywhere, or just plain sleep.

Except once. One weekend Moose took off to Halifax to see an old-time Navy pal, and I tagged on pretending I had friends there too, and took a room on Barrington Street. This city with the sailors and whores, ships, and surplus stores, where I bought me a bottle of rum that Friday night and in my room got stupid drunk. Then later, walking in the streets, approaching cabbies, sailors, and the occasional drunk like myself: "HEY WHERE C'NI GET A WOMAN HERE?" and lucky no one called a cop.

"HEY! Where can I get a woman here?"

"Fuck off, kid."

"Aaaah, you think you're pretty tough, don't you."

"Get lost I'm telling you."

"Aaaah, I bet you know some women?"

"FUCK OFF KID."

"I am, I am …"

30// On Saturday, I slept to noon, ate lobster with a headache in a restaurant down the street, and walked again. Got lost, my last night in that town, and tired walking, found a movie house and went inside and sat through *Robin Hood* with Errol Flynn! Then back to Barrington with cab and back to bed.

And Monday morning breakfast talk, with Sam back and all the guys … "I couldn't find my old school pal but met another fella in the street who took me to a dance hall and I met this broad that looked exactly like Eartha Kitt. Then back to bed HO HO HOOO!"

Moose said the dance hall sounded like the Olympic Gardens and I thought so.

ROBIN HOOD AND LITTLE JOHN AND FRIAR TUCK … FUCK.

31//   Truro, N.S.

July 20, 1959

Dear Mom and Dad:

The next time you see me you won't know me! Am I ever putting on the weight. Sam here is the best cook I've seen in ages. (That's not including you, Mom.) Add to the extra weight, a good suntan, and you would be proud of me.

Passed those exams I mentioned and understand a small raise is on the way. By the way, I took out a $1,000 Savings Bond as you suggested, and surprisingly I still have money left over to put into my old bank account.

We have been in and around Truro and several small villages this past week. Interesting scenery, but nothing like home.

If you could see the work I am doing here you'd wonder how I find the energy to study at night. Hope you are all well.

Best wishes.

Love to all,

Peter

32// My job was junior man for that first month which meant that anything to do got sent my way. I'd pick and shovel with the gang, then Dewar thinks it's time the tool car's cleaned, and off I'd go. Racking up shovels and racking up picks, throwing out the paper waste from roles of wire, repacking fuses so they won't get lost, and sweeping out the tool car clean. It's damn hot work. I built a rack for the wrenches once, and Dewar said that's damn fine work, so I fixed up crates for the rubber boots. I hung the climbing spurs along one wall, and on the other hung the small rolled wire. Lit a fire beside the track and burned up junk.

I even got to work with Sam on Friday's rush. Work starts early Friday morning, so the gang takes off at three o'clock. I'd peel Sam's spuds, and haul him water from the water car to fill his tanks. And sometimes scrub the kitchen floor, and bunk car floor, and shine the black steel stove top off with grease.

I usedta like to work with Sam. Come afternoon the work's all done, until the dishes hit the sink again. Then I'd tell Sam to go on home. "I'll do them on the weekend, Sam." So even Sam got an early start for home.

33// I should say now that meeting Ray Malone in August like I did, and letting loose the way I did, these weeks with Sam don't sound like much. And yet sometimes when I think back, I think the quiet days were best, the weekends walking on the track, or even the nights with Sam and talk. With Ray I did a lot of crazy things. A lot of things I'm likely to forget.

But I don't know. They say you soon forget those things. But I don't know. It's pretty easy to live it up, but it's not that simple living it down …

34// REPORT TO HAROLD HAY SIGNAL MAINTAINER HAMPTON NEW BRUNSWICK MONDAY AUGUST 2, 8:00 AM.

35// That transfer came in the morning mail. It's Friday after work again and washing up and off to catch the 41 with a bag of dirty underwear. I'll make it home and head back down on Sunday morning. I'm off to see my Mom and Dad. Com'on old pass. Gonna miss old Nova Scotia, but I'm going home. And on the train I fall to thinking how I've been away for more'n a month and how (thank God) my cheque came in. Payday today. Be hell to land home broke right now.

"Been saving much?"

"Oh yeah, oh yeah."

And feeling like a grown up man that Saturday and stepping off the morning train with fellas at the station there:

"Hey! How ya doin, Peter Boy?"

"Not bad, not bad."

And: "Where ya workin?"

"Halifax": I lie like hell.

Then picking up my overnight and heading down the street to home.

36// Dad standing by the stairs up to our flat: "Hey! Welcome home, boy. How've you been?"

"I'm good, I'm good": we're shaking hands.

I meet my sister on the stairs:

"What's wrong?"

"Nothin, nothin. Just came home for the weekend. Mind?"

"Oh good to see ya": running then and off on down the street to play.

Then Grandma's hugging, pushing me to sit and eat. And Mom walks in:

"Good Lord, you're thin!"

And that's what Moms are for, I tell myself, and sit down chewing on a piece of ham and asking for another egg. With all this trying to show how changed I am.

"You're starving. Don't you eat at all?"

"Not starving, Mom, I just eat more … I'm working hard."

Then: "How do you like the job?" that's Dad.

"It's doing the job." I wink at him: "I'll sure be glad to go on to school. HEY! When is Grandad in?"

Grandma: "On the Bay Train … home tonight."

"That's good, that's good. I'm working with a friend of his. I wrote about him." And tell them all about old Sam. And Grandma knows him! Met him here with Grandad years ago (I'm eating still), and Mom is digging in my overnight and moaning on the fact that I don't wash. "It's worse than when he went away to summer camp," she's telling us. "Came home that time with nothing left to wear!"

I'm laughing, trying hard to sound grown up, and tell her how she LOVES to wash my socks.

And she: "Your feet must smell damn good!"

Then finished eating, in my room, and changing shirts. I'd love to take a bath right now but Mom would scream: HE HASN'T HAD A BATH SINCE HE LEFT HOME!

That's true. The other guys go home each week. We haven't got a shower in the cars. Besides another day can't hurt me none.

I spend the afternoon with Dad. It's Saturday and Gorham's Uptown Drug Store sells root beer. We're sitting at the soda bar and laughing at a hundred things. We laugh at Grandma stuffing people with her food. She always figures you haven't had a bite in days, and every meal she dishes up is three. We laugh at Mom, her moaning on my dirty shorts, and Dad says he was just the same.

"She married me to clean me up!" We both laugh at that.

Then walk along the track together, stopping at a switch a while while I explain how automatic switches work. Surprises me! He's read about the work in *Track*, this magazine that Grandad gets.

It's three o'clock.

I show my transfer telegram to Dad. "Replacing Hay's assistant … holidays. Promotion of a sort," says I, "they only take the better guys." This pleases him. I hear him telling Mom that night.

He says I ought to take a fishing rod. The St. John River's pretty fine down there. I think I will.

Three-thirty now and back inside our unair-conditioned flat my Grandma's ferns are wilting in the summer heat. Still every day she waters them and picks the dead leaves from the pots.

It's five o'clock and sitting down to eat again, then after supper talking with my Dad again to sounds of women's work around the house. That's Grandma clicking dishes in the kitchen sink while Mom spreads out the clothes she's washed, and humming with her iron in her hand, forgets a while her son has been away.

In Campbellton, the lights come on and up and down the summer streets, a windless night wilts flowers in their dried-up beds.

"AREN'T YOU THROUGH YET?" My mother knocking on the bathroom door behind which Kate, my sister, sits. "IT TAKES THAT GIRL A WEEK TO GET TO BED," Mom moans. And one day's play sounds very weary of it all: "It's soo awful hot, Mom."

"I know, hon, but hurry, it's cooler in your room."

37// MEMORY IV: A long slow night like when you all lived home. You find it longer though, and sitting there you read the paper, two, three times, and rock in Grandad's rocking chair, where later on tonight he'll plop down weary of a railroad day. A wind-up clock on top of the stove ticks off the time. A radio in a car below reminds you that you have one here. You turn it on. Your Dad is reading in the living room. Your Mom is tucking Kate in bed. Your Grandma sits across the room and darns a big wool sock for you-know-who. You share the house, the six of you, and don't talk much.

38// I heard him coming in that night. It seemed as though I'd never been away from home; the creaking, heavy breathing on the stairs. The sigh with closing up the top step door and in the kitchen hanging up his railroad for the day. I heard him take his milk pint from his pail, then washing it and setting it away.

CALUMP CALUMP his boots are off and paper rattles as he settles in his chair. Page 1, and 2, the sports, and local news. And then his rocking chair begins to creak. He's lit his pipe. It's always wet, the pipe I mean. He doesn't care, just sucks away, then leaves his rocking chair to spit. He runs the water in the kitchen sink and sock foots back across the oilcloth to sit back down.

It's funny how those sounds come back. Just lying there in bed that night, all wide awake, I must have counted every breath. I counted every creak of that old chair. I heard him yawn that jaw-crack yawn, that HO DE HO DE HUM of his, and start to bed. I heard the kitchen light click off and heard his hand along the wall down to his room. I had a million things to say, but held my breath. I sat in bed like when I was a boy, and listened to those noises of a man. If I'd got up we coulda talked all night. I had so many things to say.

And then his mattress sags and creaks and click his bedside light goes out. He didn't even know that I was home, and many many things to say fell fast asleep.

39// The sunrise never made mornings in our house. It's not as though the night-time ends and people stretch and slowly start the day. I never knew a morning quite like that. No matter what the day might be, the holidays, or Saturdays, the Sundays, or the twenty-fourth of May, not with a yawn for me, but BANG BANG BANG the day begins. YOUR BREAKFAST'S ON THE TABLE, SEVEN O'CLOCK!

I'm yawning, stretching out, today though in my room. My bed is warm, and so unlike my railroad bunk that, Jesus,

I can hardly move. It's morning time. It's seven o'clock. There's voices in the kitchen, Mom, and Grandma singing at the stove, and sister Kate, and Dad is there. I shake myself. Then in the kitchen, MORNIN to them all. And: "Where's Grandad?"

"The call boy came around at five-thirty": Grandma tells me. "Said he'd see you next time up."

And I wanted to tell him all about the gang, about the work, and where we were. We coulda even talked about my move, and how I met my now friend Sam. But best of all I coulda heard him talk. I coulda asked him all about the railroad when. His stories woulda brought it back again. That real rail-rolling railroad's all gone now. He mighta told me how he took the troop trains down to Halifax, at dead of night, with no lights on. He coulda told me all about the Gaspé line. The roundhouse talk of a railroad man. He loved the Frenchmen on the Gaspé line. He talked about them all the time. We had so many things to say, but living in a railroad world, and working at a call boy's call, he had no time.

I'd miss this morning later on, when tired of it all and sick. I never heard him talk again.

Just two months later in Rivière Bleu that telegram came. GRANDAD PARALYZED STOP STROKE STOP DOCTOR SAYS WILL NEVER WALK AGAIN STOP CAN YOU GET HOME?

40// So far away that other Sunday now; that-off-to-church and-home-again, and sitting-down-to-chicken-stew-Sunday. And packing up my bags that day. The hugging and the shaking hands, and: "When you coming home again?"

The good intentions: "Easier to get here now. It's not as far. We'll see you soon."

And feeling when I climbed on board that train like I had never been away from home. The waving, kissing to them all, impatient for the train to go. How old's a boy before he turns a man? How old's a man?

41// Just one month later going home, all worried then, and sick and sore. Those good intentions shot to hell, for here's my first trip home since then. GRANDAD PARALYZED … CAN YOU GET HOME? And going cause I had to go. And so to dreaming back again …

42// In Hampton now and stepping off the train that day. The station in the centre part of town where sits a square, around which stand the fire hall, a white wood church, post office, and the old town hall. And while I'm standing here comes Harold Hay as big as any man I'd seen and talking slow tells me he's got a room for me, or would I care to look myself. Pronounces CARE like CAR, so when I left to go back to the gang, or meet with Ray Malone as it turned out, I heard him hollering TAY CAR YOURSELF!

That morning: "Got your bags up at my house. It's not too far. They come in on the early train."

Then walking off the longest not-too-far I ever walked, and listening: "My helper's taking holidays. Guy Cassidy. He's staying home though. Don't travel much. They got a room there. Put you up. His wife cooks good. They're right across the street from me."

The cleanest home I ever saw and many restless nights since then I've dreamed about the quiet of that little room. My bed and bookshelf, patchwork quilt, the thick wool rug. Clothes-closet and, a table lamp which I read by in the night. And daughter Janice, deep in love with some young man in old Saint John.

The two weeks working here with Harold Hay and living in that small clean town were good for me. Been in a bunk car just a bit too long and start by bathing every night, and changing underwear, and changing socks, and staying in with Cassidys at night like I was home. Then Saturday around the house and talk with Janice who was so sincere. This little girl (she's still in school) with soft brown hair, who told me I should have a girl, and with her worried brown brown eyes as much as said it should be her. That Janice I would think about when waking up in some strange bed, in some strange town, all sick and lost, and all confused.

It's Hampton where I learned to drive a motorcar, and working on the track toward Saint John, I'd sit proud on that hardwood yellow seat all happy then, and where the track and roadside met, I'd wave to people walking or in cars. It's Hampton where I felt the railroad in my bones. It's not a job … not just a job … the railroad's gotta be a part of you!

I'm learning things with Harold Hay. By two weekends I think I've maybe made the grade. I'm one up on the new guys now and engineers come from the ranks. I'll get me better jobs to do.

I learn to check the battery tubs that keep the signals winking at the trains. I learn to drive the motorcar. I learn to change a signal lamp and take a reading on a coded track. I learn that if you don't take lunch you quit at four. I smell seniority and almost write a letter home.

43// And Hampton nights were Janice and the stiff-back chairs. Her Mom and Dad next door perhaps, or in the kitchen playing Hearts. Big sofa here which we both feel but never dare to think about. And so we sit, both talking in those stiff-back chairs. But once, just once, I catch her in a half-play hug, and feel it there. In both of us. She's young but hungry in a frightened way. And so we talk.

She tells me all about her boy, so cautiously, and always in a temporary way, half-hinting that it could be me. She hopes to be engaged someday, but first she'll have to finish school. Three kids would make her happy too. I tell her how I might go on to university. She half-thinks she might like to teach, but nursing doesn't cost as much.

And Hampton is a TV football game:

"I used to play in high school," says I.

"How many people on a team?"

"Fifteen if I remember right."

And leaving later on that week while she's at school, I find a letter in my bedside book:

Dear Peter:

I guess it is hard for you to understand how I can be so much in love. Don is a wonderful boy. I wish you had been able to meet him. You would have gotten along well. Maybe someday you will meet someone somewhere and you will understand what I was trying to tell you. I hope you do. It will be a lucky day for both of you. All the best to you Peter.

Luv,

Janice

P.S., I asked my Dad about the football. There are twelve people on a team. Did you really play?

44//   Ah, Janice! Stay the way you are.

45//   TOOT TOOT … TAY CAR YOURSELF! … and off to Moncton and to find the gang, all rested now, and ready for the work ahead. The Hamptons in this world of ours are real hometowns.

46//   MONCTON, NEW BRUNSWICK: arriving there with bits of Janice in my head and bits of Hampton and the small hometowns you dream about; arriving there all happy now and dying for a chance to do my stuff.

I feel the railroad in my bones today. I'm railroad now. And in the office asking for my gang, and there's the guy said engineers come from the ranks.

"One second now."

Me standing there, this office full of pretty girls with papers scattered all around, not looking though, but busy at a thousand things; no time for me.

"Ah here it is!" And tells me that the gang is here in town, but adding like he just found out, that I've been moved.

"Transferred I guess … "

"Where?" And waiting while he reads some more.

"Ah here it is!" Then pausing: "You … are joining Eddie Linden's gang. And they are up in … Edmundston."

KEEERIST!

"That's quite a trip," he laughs at me. "One second now": and out he goes to check with someone in another room. Then coming back: "Ah, here we are!" And tells me I'm to finish out this week first, here in town. "Your gang is sided by the shops … okay?"

"Okay."

And outside walking by the tracks there's shops as far as I can see. What goddamn shops? And stop to tell station cop what I've been told.

"The Signal Shops?" he says: "Maybe?" That goddamn cop.

It's three o'clock in Moncton now and feeling just a bit let down I find the cars parked by the signal shops and drop my bag in on my bunk.

"HI SAM!"

"WELL I'LL BE DAMNED: MY BOY'S COME HOME!"

"But not for long": I laugh at him. (I'm trying to hide how bad I feel.) "I'm transferred up to Edmundston. I just got word—"

"When?"

"Monday morning so they say": and tell him how I'm here till then, and then sit down to eat a while with Sam and doughnuts and a cup of hot black tea.

"The gang is ten miles up the track … siddown siddown."

And eating more.

"What gang you on?"

And tell him what I've just been told: "It's Eddie Linden? London's? gang."

And Sam shouts: "HEY NOW, GOOD FOR YOU! HEY SHIT! HEY HO! YOU'RE GONNA BE WITH RAY MALONE!"

"Who's Ray Malone?"

"WHO'S RAY MALONE!"

"Yeah who?"

"He's … well he's … hell he's just about the best damn guy you'll ever know. He's just the kinda guy you need to meet. He's worked the best gangs anywhere. You MUSTA heard me mention him! He worked here coupla months ago … before you came. AH PETE, this move was made for you! It's what you need! It's the best damn thing that ever happened to you! It's … JESUS CHRIST, IT'S FOUR O'CLOCK!"

And laughing then and pitching in with Sam, for suppertime is coming up, and listening to Ray Malone, as told by Sam. And seeing him … Big Ray Malone, though later finding out I'm wrong, and not because of Sam at all, but more because imagination got the best of me.

That same wild thinking in the weeks to come made Ray Malone what I thought then, with Sam I mean. Cause Sam knew Railroad Ray Malone and never saw him any other way. And Ray Malone was woolly wild and tromped on everyone he could. "LET'S YOU AND ME GO FUCK SOME FROGS," I'd hear him say all through Quebec. And Ray would bring them to the cars, all drunk at night; women who thought the bunk cars safe from home. He'd fuck them good and laugh at them and walk them home, and then come back and laugh some more. He'd drink with husbands in the hotel bars and meet their wives on the track outside. He did it all so slick and good that no one ever thought or knew. And EVERYONE loved Ray Malone. And I did too.

47// I wonder where old Ray's today?

48// I'm cutting carrots, railroad-style, and plopping them in one big pot, and sitting on a bench beside the stove. Here's Sam, walking up the floor; the icebox, stove, the table, and the sink. He's big but knows his kitchen well. I'm sitting there and all amazed I watch the smoothness of it all. No wasted steps. No wasted time. Big Sam, with little housewife ways, is hard at work.

Potatoes on the stove at four, and boiling now. The carrots get a hot spot next. And scraping off the grill for chops he starts the water for the tea. The table set, and Sam sits down and, running through his super-head, the supper that he's done a thousand times. Amazing me the more that day by talking to me all the while.

He's gabbing on and building up the life of Ray Malone. The bigness, brashness of it all. The tiny, almost meaningless detail. The laughing, singing Ray Malone that everyone loves. The sometimes sad and lonely Ray Malone. (Though this I never got to see.) The always Ray Malone, alone unless you want to be his friend and follow him. The working, never-stopping Ray Malone whose motto was YOU WORK TO EARN YOUR PLAY and lived that way. The ONE, the ONLY, RAY MALONE. It's Thursday night and Sam has got me anxious to be there.

PART 3

49//   I hadn't yet met Ray Malone but had another friend back then, though not a railroadman. And weekends when my Dad would pay the fare, and two since starting on this job, I'd catch a train and head for Shediac. Spent many a weekend drinking on the beach, and many a weekend I just didn't get back.

Hello Jim Solomon!

Here was my first away-from-home and madman friend. He used to live in my hometown, but now he ran a music store. And like I said, I'd catch a train and land in town (that's Moncton where I am right now) and walk along the crowded Friday Night streets, straight to the Moncton Record Room. And here I'd lie, and Jim'd stretch the truth a bit, until at last I came to be King of the Railroad Bums.

Here, Bible in my hand, if drunk enough, or some mad book I'd never read, and dressed in jeans and a dirty shirt, I'd read to Jim's new Moncton friends. Or if I met him at the store, he'd close the store and off we'd go to Shediac and a cottage he had there where we could drink. There we had beer, and food, and solitude, except of course from the curious gang that dropped around to see Jim's friend. And Jim had a typewriter, long since gone, and I had parts of what became this book. And the funniest thing of all was Jim, who'd typed a page from Kerouac's *On the Road* which he'd show people who came to call. And there we'd sit and drink our beer (though neither of us were old enough); and never a night went by alone.

To do the things Jim said I'd done, I'd have to live a hundred years. A merchant seaman, lumberjack, an artist, and a bum; one week I'd just got back from New Orleans, then San Francisco'd been my home. My real home just two hundred miles, and somehow no one ever knew.

Those weekends between Jim and me, became Ray Malone and me, and that day knowing that I'd soon be gone, I talked with Sam and planned the wildest one of all. It's Thursday night and suppertime. It's Moncton and I just got back. It's four more days to meeting Ray Malone. It's just about five o'clock.

50// I don't know how he did it, but he did. I didn't lose a damn day's pay. I'm talking when we hear the gang come in. And then I heard them lifting off the motorcars. "GEDDOUDA HERE ... GOWAN I'LL SEND YOUR STUFF TO EDMUDSTON. I'LL FIX IT SO YOU WON'T LOSE ANY PAY. YOU NEED A HOLIDAY. NOW GET!"

And out the cook car door, not looking back, and jumping frogs and switches down the track, and crawling under cars as fast's I can, and all steamed up. Been on the railroad more'n a month and still got more'n a year to go. Besides I need a holiday. So what the hell! I stop just at the freight yard edge to brush the railroad dirt away and catch my breath. I guess I'd told Sam all about Jim. We used to sit and talk at night.

So thank you, Sam.

You leave the station yard in Moncton, New Brunswick, head west on any one of the streets facing you, and after three or four blocks you come to St. George Street which runs parallel to Main Street where the station is. So there I go on a Thursday night, all rested now, and rich with a pay cheque just picked up two days ago. It's me'n I'm free'n I'm looking for some fun!

51// Strange people in the Moncton Record Room all picking up the latest hits and some of them laughing with Jim who looks real good as always in his corduroys and thin strip tie. He's grinning at some teenage girl and winking through his green eye glasses. He sees me coming through the door and the stage is set for a joke so old to Jim and me that we wonder now just why it works the way it does.

"Can I help you?"

"Yes, I'd like a dozen eggs, two quarts of milk, and a pint of oysters."

People smiling, watching, waiting for one of us to laugh, while Jim and I, having done this so often, run through the routine so seriously that slowly the smiles disappear, and people stare.

"One minute please."

And out he goes to the small back room that serves as office-warehouse for the store, and comes back in. The people watching closer now as Jim, with grocery-clerk finesse, wraps up the lot.

"There you are. That will be $2.15."

Then handing him a ten buck bill and picking up my change and out. Outside, around the store, and in the back. I watch him through the curtain there, me seated at his old wood desk, and marvel at the way he carries on. The people being waited on refuse to ask.

52// It's six o'clock and locking up the store front door he yells at me: "YOU'RE GETTING BETTER ALL THE TIME!" And then the sitting back to laugh. And laughing harder at an hour of foolish talk and things we've done together and away. Been just about a month since I was here, so bring each other up to date. Then close the store and head for the cottage and Shediac with promises like: "Just you wait!" and, "What a weekend this will be!" And driving there in Jim's old Oldsmobile, we talk some more.

"And how's the railroad?"

"Good, Jim, Good." And tell him all about my move, and all about Big Ray Malone.

"I got your note from Hampton just last week. This Janice sounds like quite a dish!"

I think back then to Janice and the stiff-back chairs, remembering the letter now and all I'd said. Jim drives and waits to hear the rest. I make it up to laugh with him, the long hot nights, her Mom and Dad away, or sleeping in the next damn room! I tell him how she cried the day I left, and how she said she'd never let another man touch her until I came back. We laugh like hell. That's funny when you're seventeen.

And at the cottage eating now and getting set to go for beer. The stores are closed but this is bootleg country, just before the bars went in. The canteens all along the road sell beer. And advertise! Big signs on top of all these canteens read: LOBSTER 67 CENTS, LOBSTER 66 CENTS, LOBSTER 65 CENTS. Can't tell you how they educate the tourist trade, but everybody here knows what it means. It's beer! Those prices mean the goddamn beer; and just in case you ever buy, they don't sell pints.

Old Jim and I, we drive awhile, then settle for the 65. I buy us twelve quarts. So does Jim. And off we go. We tried to get some lobster too, but the guy had none; just beer in big brown paper bags. We load it in the car and go.

Here's Pointe du Chêne, just two miles south of Shediac, where finally we stop to drink. Been laughing, talking since we left the store (the Music Store). Old Oldsmobile parked in the sand, with Jim and I sprawled on the beach, is covered with that east coast mud, and has been used for just what we are doing so many times, that one of Jim's Moncton friends, Edgar Hachey, or lonesome Eddie Kerwin, has nicknamed it the Picnic Basket.

53// "And how's the railroad, really though": Jim knowing how this whole year came about (way back before I came down here. I knew him then.) And so keen on my taking up the job: "You'll be the only railroadman I know!" All sounding just a bit too much like me that June day in the kitchen back at home, and telling Dad: "The Railroad's what I need all right. A year away from school will do me good. And think of it, the Railroad Dad! The work and all the training too!"

Jim sounding so much like me, in fact, that had it not been for his great love of flashy suits and thin strip ties, I think he might have joined up too.

So: "How's the railroad, really though?"

"It's good, Jim, good. And Christ, I'm dying to meet this Ray Malone. I've never been to Edmundston, and Sam says Ray Malone is worth the trip." I'd told Jim all about old Sam.

"I've been there once": says he, and scribbles out a name for me.

"You look her up and say hello. You going back to school next year?" Reminding me I have to write a letter home.

"Oh yeah."

And: "How's the book?"

"Not bad. Slow though."

For this is the year of Kerouac and the Beat Generation, and Jim and I, having read one or two books by one or two of these mad boy men, had decided earlier this same summer that since the young men of America were getting so much praise about and for so many of the things we were doing ourselves right here in backwoods New Brunswick, we too would write books about it all.

And drinking on like this for three whole hours, not like today when sleep sets in, but with that straight-gut, teenage energy that fathers envy in their sons; still, getting drunker all the while, and sitting on the night-time beach, and scheming on the night ahead.

It's ten o'clock. Twelve quarts of beer are gone.

"We get some more?"

"Okay": and off we go to get us twelve more quarts; not needing them with twelve more in the car right now, but buying them because we think it's fun. Jim joking with the girl back there: "Twelve more quarts of lobster, please!" Then driving to the cottage, and the phone. Jim phoning, talking, laughing there, and trying hard to find us two fine girls to join the fun; though knowing all the while, as I do too, that every single one is back in town. It's Thursday night.

54//   At 10:00 AM, I'm up again, with giant hard-on and a big headache, staggering the cottage floor, wondering if Jim got to work on time, and looking for a fresh, clean shirt. The sun is up on a hot hot day and kids are screaming down along the beach. I sit a while in the sun, then back indoors I find some paper and I write:

Moncton, N.B.
August 13, 1959

Dear Mom and Dad:

Have just finished up my two weeks in Hampton and, as a matter of fact, have been on the railroad over a month and a half. I hope you are all well. You will notice that I am in Moncton once again. Been here two days, filling out forms, and getting ready for what should be as big a surprise to you as it was to me—a transfer—to Edmundston! No definite word yet, but I understand the time just spent in Hampton was meant to be a sort of training session for me and that now I am going on to something a little better than my present work. I don't know yet what it will mean in dollars and cents, but am sure it will be something. By the way, my bank account (or University Fund) is looking good.

I sometimes think back to my boyhood dreams of being a big railroadman, especially an engineer, and see how childish I was. I ...

I stopped that letter there and walked outdoors, then down along the sand road to the beach. The railroad so far's not that bad. Oh sure, I laugh it off with Mom and Dad: I'M GOING BACK TO SCHOOL NEXT YEAR ... A YEAR OF THIS IS LOTS FOR ME! I do the same damn thing with Jim from time to time. I'm not ashamed of what I do. The money's good.

55// Some mother calls her little girl inside. I must look mad.

56// JIM'S BACK and telling me to hustle now. He's got clean shirts and a pair of pants for me and off we go. Before we leave he waits for me to X out that last paragraph, and jot down quick:

Will write you when I get to Edmundston.

Love to all,
Peter

57// "So how'd you spend the afternoon?"

"I slept a lot."

"You writing to your Mom and Dad?"

"Yeah, stop so I can get a stamp."

"You should be working on the book."

"I'll put the letter in the book."

"Hey! That's a good idea though."

"I haven't had a goddamn thing to eat."

"You hungry?"

"Yeah, but I think it's too late."

"Hey! Don't die in my car!"

"Why?"

"Because."

"Because why?"

"Because you'll stink, that's why. Hey! How do you tell the groom at a French wedding?"

"How?"

"He's the one in the clean bowling shirt!"

And so it goes, the two of us, all drunk with nothing left

to do. It's Friday night. We're driving into Moncton from the shore. Jim's got a date, and me one too. He says I've met her once before:

"You met her at a beach house dance."

"The one with the pout?"

"That's not a pout. She's got naturally curly lips!"

58// And so it goes, the weekend, two of us, and crates of beer. The two of us, as Jim would say, with nothing left to talk about. MONCTON, 1959: I signed up here, and like I said, came back whenever I got the chance, to visit Jim and plan big weekends, like the one just done, that never seemed to leave the ground. These weekends proving, though, what Dad once said: "When two good friends get together, they don't have to DO anything. All that matters, Peter," he said, "is that they get a chance to borrow from each other, a little of that special something each sees in the other—a little of that special something each is certain makes the other the greatest person in the world."

And that's the way it was with me. Me watching Jim, then heading back to work all filled with fight. I'M GONNA WORK. I'M GONNA SAVE. THERE'S NOT A GODDAMN THING THAT I CAN'T DO.

I think it was the same with Jim.

59// We had a GREAT BIG talk, as Jim would say, before I left; inside the station, Jim and me. It's Sunday and the weekend's gone. I told him how I hadn't saved a goddamn cent; not one damn cent, despite my crazy letters home. And how, to save a lot of fight, I'd kept the college dream alive, with talk of going back to school, for Mom and Dad. And how, even then, I didn't know myself what might be best. I told him stories I had heard back home, from Grandad and the section men, of how the railroad made a damn fine wife, of how the work, and people that you met, would keep you young. I told him stories from my railroad home as told to me, or overheard; the stories that had put me here, and got me walking on the track: BIG RAILROADMAN! Seventeen-years-old and trying hard to fill my Grandad's railroad boots. So all fired up then telling Jim, the RAILROAD as it was to me, and was and would be ... second hand. I wondered to him why it was that people looked on labour with a sneer. And prophesied I'd likely end up going back to school and all, but wondered why. You finish school to go to work, so why not keep on working now? The money's good.

And on like this for just about an hour, until, like always, as the train pulls in, we're talking off each other's ears. With just ten minutes left to go we think about a million things to say.

Jim talking now, and wondering, and telling me to take

my time, and pointing out my letters home don't hurt at all.
"You're lucky, you're away from Home … I had to do the
same thing There!"

Jim talking now: "You still have more'n a year to go!"
And telling me: "The railroad's lotsa fun I know … but SAVE
SOME MONEY, JESUS CHRIST … be HELL to change your mind next
fall, and have to work another year!"

TOOT TOOT … aaboaard.

"I'll write you when I get there."
"Good … you got that number?"
"Yeah."
"Good Luck! And say hello to Ray Malone!"
"I will, I will."

Then on the train.

60//   "You still have more'n a year to go!" That's Jim's
Okay … that's Jim's solution to the whole damn thing … his
one big answer to the what I'm gonna do! I'M WASTING TIME …
I GOTTA MAKE MY MIND UP SOON … and all I needed was a word
from you.

Been more'n a month of railroad now, of working in the
sun all day, of Sam and my big appetite, of drinking beer and

having me a damn good time; been more'n a month away
from home, away from school, and still don't see the point
of going back. FORGET IT. DROP IT: tell myself, but still keep
thinking how it's gonna be:

LOOK DAD IT'S JUST NO GODDAMN USE! THERE'S SOME OF US
ARE MEANT FOR SCHOOLS, AND SOME OF US ARE MEANT TO WORK.
I KNOW YOU PLANNED ON UNIVERSITY, AND MOM DID TOO ... BUT
LISTEN NOW ...!

HO HO HO!

"Your ticket please."
"Pass ... Edmundston ..."
"Thank you."

61//   And so to thinking on the train, of this, and many
other things. Of Grandad. Who his father was. And then of
meeting Ray Malone.

The smell of oranges in the train dry air ... two sailors, drunk
since Halifax, are heading home ... two kids with Mommy,
watching them ... one drinking Coke, the other eating
an orange, peelings scattered underneath his seat ... oranges
in my Grandad's jampacked lunchpail ... and me in jeans
and a dirty shirt ... Hope Sammy gets my luggage there ...

And sleeping off and on. It's time to eat. And sleeping off and on again until it's dark.

62//   MEMORY V: Almost gone, the kids who want to drive these trains. Except in families linked like boxcars in their railroad homes … COME FROM A LONG LINE OF RAILROADERS! Shunted out of schools across this railroad earth, some on their own steam, standing through an unemployment line, sticking out their chests and flexing throttle-hungry hands and all struck blind on a one-track mind to hear the steel on steel of engine wheels and feel the pull of two-mile lines of freight upon their backs … just somehow crying for a weird swing-shift and pounding callboy on a sleeping railroad door. August on the railroad earth and all goes well.

63//   Ah well … and thinking back to Jim again: You still have more'n a year to go … you still have more'n a year to go … you still have more'n a year to go you still have more'n a year to go youstillhavemore'nayeartogo … and then to sleep.

PART 4

64// Now let's go back to the sight of me, all warm in bed, and horny too, and waking up from time to time to feel her breathing next to me. Fifteen years old. My little girl is sleeping now. Old bunk car creaking on the track. No sound outside except the rain. I'm sick from drink, and thinking about that telegram: GRANDAD PARALYZED ... CAN YOU GET HOME? And falling back to sleep again, with big hard-on, and an aching head. It's Friday night (or Saarday now, as Ray would say); in any case, it's Rivière Bleu.

She wakes up too from time to time, and touches me. Her hands are hot. She sleeps with them between her legs. She kisses me, her big wet, sleepy mouth against my neck. My arms, and legs, around her now, (she's small), and hugging her to keep us warm. Then falling off to sleep again, her hands on me.

65// Frog-stickin, Ray called it. And every after-supper night he'd stand there at the old tin sink and wash himself, and splash from head to feet with aftershave, and brush his teeth (with salt or soda if he had no paste); right through Quebec. He'd squeeze his big old blackhead nose, and bare his gums, and then he'd turn to grin at me:

"I'm sumthin, ain't I really though?"

"You sure's hell are!"

Then pointing at the washstand say: "It's all yours boy, but hustle now."

And so I'd wash while Ray sat on his bunk, or stood around and tuned his banjo for the night ahead:

> A frog wenta courtin and he did go
> uh huh
> A frog wenta courtin and he did go
> uh huh
> A frog wenta courtin and he did go
> A lookin for a English girl to call his own
> uh huh uh huh uh huh

Then out the door and down the track: in Edmundston

and St. Hilaire, at Caron Brook, Courchesne, and Rivière Bleu, in Sully and St. Eleuthère, in Monk, and once in old Quebec. Big Ray and me in French hotels, all drunk and swinging up a storm; two table-hoppers in the hotel bars, with people yelling to buy us beer.

Ray talking for the two of us, I don't talk French, and telling jokes

"She says she thinks you're cute."

"Tell her I think she's cute too."

And watching her expression change as Ray translates what I've just said, and knowing by the laughter then he's made it up.

"Hey what'd you tell her?"

"Never mind!"

"Com'on what'd you tell her?" grabbing Ray in mock attack, and laughing too, then slowing down to sing again, or drink more beer. The people everywhere know Ray, he's worked this line for two, three years, all through Quebec. His French he learned along the track, it's bad but exciting French; you can tell the way the Frenchmen here listen closely and laugh at him and shake their heads.

66// Frog-stickin, Ray called it, as back we'd stumble to the cars at night with girls or women from the hotel bar. Two women and a bag of beer. They'd buy the beer. It's Friday night, or Saturday, it's weekend and the gang's gone home.

"TWO LOVELY WOMEN AND A BOG OF BEER": Ray'd yell, and slap one on the ass, and grin at me.

67// So this night quite a treat for me, and there I am not too too drunk, but happy like a goddamn fool; you're more my age I'm telling her. And kissing her and talking fast, though she can't understand a word and all the while feel each other up and understand. We stumble on the ties and laugh. Off come her shoes. I carry her. I put her down. We feel some more.

Fifteen years old: I tell myself: and pretty too. She's got the biggest black French eyes.

And there's the bunk car sitting on the track. She can't say no, I tell myself. She might think we're just on a walk! God no! So feel her more direct this time. She won't say no. And kiss her on her big wet mouth.

68// Next morning, like I said before, the SCREAMING, kicking, wakes me up; the SHOUTING, CURSING, all in French, and me in bed. I can't fight back. I can't get up. Got nothing on. My arms protect my face and head. I yell at Ray: "GET HER THE HELL OFFA ME! GET HER OUTA HERE."

And there's Big Ray, grabbing, pulling, talking in this

woman's ear (he too in French) until the whole thing becomes so hideous, so wild, that I think for sure I must be dreaming, and I try to wake up.

This woman is mad, about forty years old, and out to kill me in my bed. She's bare feet in her slip and bra, her hair's all matted on one big cheek. There's lipstick smeared around her chin.

And there's my girl. My little girl. She's yelling too. She's crying, pulling on her skirt, one hand too busy at a flood of tears:

"MAMA MAMA MAMA … MAMAAAA!"

And Mama stops to yell at her. My little girl. And turns away from me at last.

And there I go!

69// All bare ass scared, but quick as shit, I made it to the bunk car door and jumped outside cutting my feet in the limestone trackbed, but I ran like hell, with Mama cursing after me before I hit the goddamn ground. There were twenty cars on our siding and I ran, and I limped, and I didn't look back, from our car (almost in the middle of the line), down to the other end. My head was aching and I had no clothes.

Ten cars away I dared look back. Mama's inside. I hear her yelling at Ray Malone. And there I wait for a long long time and then limp back along the ditch. I remember thinking how lucky I was. The siding might have been in town.

70// FROG-STICKIN, Ray called it. Lotsa fun!

71// You shouldn't think at times like this. I know that now. But sitting there I thought a lot. I thought about jails, and whips, and screaming—thought about trying to get an English lawyer who might sympathize with my case. I even thought about running off into the woods where I might become a sort of backwoods, Quebec Tarzan. I brushed my feet off with a wad of grass and thought some more. WHY DON'T THEY GO? WHY DON'T THEY GET ON OUTA HERE?

I don't know how it started, or what made me think it would do any good (me a Protestant in the middle of Quebec), but suddenly I began to make all sorts of promises; to myself at first, and then to God. God-honest promises, like:

HOLY GOD, if you can hear me now. If you're the same God I had when I went to Sunday School in Campbellton, New Brunswick, then maybe you remember me. I know I haven't been the best person in the world, but there are lots worse than I am. God, if I can just get in that bunk car and get my clothes and get out of Rivière Bleu without any trouble, I'll change. I'll stop lying to my parents. They aren't really lies anyway, you know. I just try to make them happy. I just try to be the inventor of good news for them.

GOD, I didn't mean to take that little girl to bed. HONEST. It must have been the beer in me, and if I can just get out of here without any trouble I'll stop that too … and I'll start to save my money and I'll go to university next year and make everyone proud of me.

72// I'd never been that scared before (and never since). I stopped praying for awhile to wonder if there was an English God and a French God, and if there was, would my God even be listening in Quebec. And the more I prayed, the more I thought, and the more I thought, the more scared I got. And I shivered in the morning cold for a long long time. I'm three cars down from where I jumped, and now I can't hear anything; so think some more, and then remember Grandad and the telegram again … O GOD, if I can just get home and see my Grandad, everything will be all right. I know I could have been going home every weekend. I've just been too busy having a good time for myself. I'll go home now … HONEST.

And then at last I hear the bunk car door, and Ray then talking in a normal voice, and Mama too. There, crouching in behind the boxcar wheels, I see them starting down the track. My little girl and old Mama. I limp up to the ditch-side door, and back inside.

"YOU GET YOUR ASS ON OUT OF HERE": that's Ray Malone. "SHE SAYS SHE'S GONE TO GET THE COPS I'D FLY IF I WAS YOU

I MEANIT PACK YOUR GODDAMN BAGS AND GET WE'LL MOVENA COUPLA DAYS. YOU JOIN US THEN. I'll say you're sick and took off home." And Ray's as scared as I am now, but this is good. I couldna taken a kidding then. And there's the two of us on fire, digging in my locker for my clothes and stuffing up my suitcase on the floor and all the while Ray talking fast and scared: "You shoulda heard her SCREAM when she woke up. You left the little slut's shoes right here beside the door when you hauled her up the ladder last night. She spotted them as soon as she rolled over this mornin and was outa bed like a whore in a raid. JESUS, JESUS, DID SHE GO!"

So out I go and down the track, my shoes hurting on my poor cut feet; my suitcase heavy with a hundred things I didn't need. And all the while praying I make it to the station and get on the train and out of town before the cops show up. And waving back to Ray Malone who's leaning out the bunk car door and looking past me down the track for signs of them. It's wet and looks like rain again. I'm hungry and my head is sore.

I catch the train and find a seat away down back. It seems like hours sitting here. Conductors walking back and forth, and people getting on for Edmundston, and there I am all set to run, all tense and watching for a uniform. And thinking like a cop I think MY HAIR! That goddamn hair routine, and find a washroom door not locked, so jump inside and comb out all my pubic hair and wash my cock and clean out all my fingernails and wash my face and open up my shirt and smell ... PERFUME! And lather up my chest with railroad soap and wash it clean, and wipe it dry, and smile in the mirror, twist my face to wake it up.

73//   Now Tuesday's payday and I won't be here to get my cheque, so I'll go on through to Moncton first and pick it up, and then go home. I'll get to Moncton late tonight and get my cheque tomorrow morning. THEN go home ... I find my telegram and read again. God, Grandad, I'm coming home. And sitting in my seat like this. The train pulls out. GOODBYE, MAMA. GOODBYE, FIFTEEN. And off again ...

"Your ticket please."
"Pass ... Moncton ...."
"On Saturday?"
"Just got a wire here last night ... transferred."
"Okeedoke, just checking."

I can't go home without a cent. I'll have to pick my cheque up first. GODDAMN THE LUCK ... those muddy little black high heels ... right by the door. Train roaring on to Edmundston. GODDAMN THE LUCK.

74//　EDMUNDSTON: I have a collect call from a Mr. Peter ——.
Will you accept the charges? Thank you. Go ahead please.

"Hello Dad?"

"Hello ...."

"Dad ..."

"Where are you?"

"How's Grandad?"

"I think he's going to be all right. Where are you?"

"I'm in Rivière Bleu and I can't get away until the boss
gets back and gives me a pass."

"When?"

"Monday."

"You'll be home Monday?"

"Yeah ... How's Grandma?"

"She's okay ... you be careful ... take your time."

"Yeah ... Grandad's gonna be okay though?"

"I think he'll be all right."

"Okay we'll see you Monday."

"Good ... be careful."

"Goodbye now."

"We'll see you Monday."

75//　Then back out on the train and off again. I'll get my
cheque before it goes out to the gang. I'll be okay. And resting
now and feeling safe ...

76// Poor Ray Malone back there alone. Just like he'd say: I'm Ray Malone, and I'm all alone. That's the way I like it. Saying that more because it rhymed than anything. And saying it even when I was with him. He liked to say that. I'm Ray Malone and I'm all alone. The cops are there for sure by now … I wonder though. And Christ you'd never know she's just fifteen. Three hours on the train and feeling safe, and giddy now. She's no damn virgin that's for sure. Her mother too. Imagine that. God, Ray was scared … and more than me …

77// September 2, 1959: I wrote a letter on the train with paper from a trainman and a stamp and put it in a railroad envelope and mailed it in the Moncton yard. I walk up town. It's Saturday (Head Office closed) and night-time too. I walk to Jim's, but no one's home, so back downtown. I'm hungry and I haven't got a cent. And then remember Sammy's cars, so to the freight yard. There's no lights on around the shops except the one-eyed signal lamps; some short, some tall (dwarfs they call the little ones), all blinking in the nighttime dark. There's nothing moving anywhere. There's station cops but none in sight. TRACK 1, TRACK 2, TRACK 3, TRACK 4, and red lights winking everywhere. Can't see my feet it's so dark here, and stepping over rails, and under cars, I look around for Sam's cook house on wheels. It's quiet here and on the far side of the yard, a shunter works at making up a train.

78// The switch stands look like people on the track at night, and look weird too with lamp-top, black and bulbous heads. No lanterns in the switch stands now. The yard is automatic, but the switch stands have been left standing anyway, with black dead heads.

79// And scare me too when climbing out from underneath a car I come up at the feet of one. But laughing nervously: I'm not afraid.

And in around the shops I go, so hungry now, and tired too. It must be after midnight now. There's bunk cars here, but not Sam's though, and all locked up. I check them, six of them, and all locked up. That's good and means there's no one here. And I have keys, my railroad keys for railroad locks. And find a cook car on the end, and up, inside.

Carnation milk, and canned tomatoes, peaches, pears, bacon, butter (light another match), and lettuce, three puddings, and a case of juice. I light more matches and prepare a feast: Big glass of juice and a bowl of stewed tomatoes (cold) with lots of salt, a can of peaches for dessert, and try to drink that milk but can't. (It's good in tea.) The pudding's all dried up and hard, so put it back. And eat away.

Just starting on my peaches in the dark when: "WHO'S IN THERE? IS ANYBODY IN THERE?"

Freeze ….

"HELLO?"

And don't dare breathe ….

"ARE YOU THE COOK?"

Still holding breath ….

"C'NYA SPARE A LITTLE BITE OF GRUB … HEY COOK?"

A goddamn bum, a railyard bum, so to the door and still half scared: "C'mon inside. But QUIET, Christ! You want the cops to pick you up?"

Can barely see him in the dark; he's small and sorta railroad grey, and all topped off with dirt grey hair. He climbs inside: "Are you the cook?"

"No … uh … I'm the cookee."

"YA GOTNO LIGHTS?"

"We're not supposed to use them on the weekends … Fire!"

"You got no tea then?"

"No … You want some juice."

"Okay. But I'd just as soon have tea COUGH COUGH."

And sitting there I hear him finish off the juice. I light a match and open up a can of pears: Here, eat these too. And hear him smack and drinking from the can and COUGHing COUGHing with each bite.

"THE COOKEE, EH?" He's watching me. "COUGH COUGH. You sure you didn't bust in here."

"No! I got keys for Jesus sakes."

"Okay. You gotno smokes?"

"Don't smoke."

He takes a package from his shirt and lights one up: "I GADAMNEARLY BROKE MY NECK."

"How'd you do that?"

"Ya jest can't hoppem anymore ... gotta get on before they start. TOOK A DIRTY GADDAMN FLIP": and stuck two scabby hands at me. "HERE FEEL ...."

"They cut?"

"They cut ... I GADDAMNEARLY BROKE MY NECK! Time they hit the yard limit they're goin like hell. I skinned my fuckin knees up too": and rolled his pant leg up for me. "TWO SCABBY KNEES. YOU SEE? YOU SEE?"

"You gotta get on before they start": I echoed his advice and he agreed.

"BUT EVERYWHERE'S A FUCKIN RAILROAD COP."

"Yeah SSHHHHHH, you'll have them here if you talk too loud."

"One time I'd soonas ride a freight than drink": he prophesied his time to come. And kept on talking in a crazy kind of way.

"THE COOKEE, EH?"

80//   And I got wishing he had made that train. And then got back here bragging about his trip. And I even got wishing we had met before, and thinking about the stories he could tell. And he kept on talking, so I got us two more cans of pears and I wished that I could write it down so someday in libraries across Canada, maybe in the middle of winter, old railroadmen, or even palsied hobos stepping indoors to warm their sleepless bodies would read it:

> PUDDLE, James Edward (1909-1977): Last known Canadian to "hop" a moving freight train outside a freight-yard limit. (See Railroad, Canadian: Facts, Figures, and History: Introduction of Diesel Power: Last Days of Steam.)

or something like that.

81//   GODDAMNIT JIMMY YOU SHOULDA MADE THAT TRAIN!

82//   "WASSAT HEY WHAT HEY ..."
"Jesus Christ don't go to sleep!"

83//   And sitting there, the two of us, I felt damn good. He's talking now, and I wish to hell Grandad was here, and

Ray Malone. Old Ray would sing this guy a railroad song, and Grandad tell us stories too. So I tell Jim Puddle about friend Ray in Rivière Bleu, and poke him now and then to wake him up. And then I tell him about the girl and how it happened yesterday and how this isn't really my cook car, and how I just now found it here, and got inside, with railroad keys, and everything comes spilling out.

And I'll be damned if he didn't laugh, and he told me all about some girl he had, right here in town. He lived with her, and how he took off now and then for some place else. I told him how I'm headed home and let him read my telegram and told him Grandad was an engineer. And told him I was broke and all and had to find my old Friend Jim and how I'd have to wait for Monday for my cheque and how I had no place to sleep.

"You should sleep here."

"No. Jesus Christ. The gang's due back."

"You'd be up. You'd be gone before they got here. Clean up the cans and lock it up. No one'll know."

"KEERIST. I'd hate like hell to get caught."

"Gawaan ... you gotta key to the bunkcar right?"

"Yeah but hell ..."

"Gawaan ..." and grabs the keys from me and opens up the other car. "YOU SEE. There's eight gaddamn beds there. The gaddamn noise will wake you up. Gawaan. Gawaan."

"And where the hell you gonna sleep?"

"Hell, I'll sleep here. I'll wake you up!"

And so to bed, or rather flopping there in all my clothes. But cleaning up the kitchen first so no one knows. And dreaming on my back awhile about this day. I get my cheque on Monday, head for home, and there I'll be. And like Ray said, the gang will move and I can join them farther on. He'll tell the foreman I'm gone home. He knows about the telegram. I wonder if she got the cops. Hell, she was there. But Ray was scared. I wonder where old Jim can be? Old Still-Have-More'n-a-Year-to-Go; he's right you know. I'll start to save my pay cheques now. He warned me way back in July. In letters too. September now. I wonder where in hell he's gone. It's Sunday now. It must be after two o'clock. I'll get the cheque on Monday ... buy myself a clean sport shirt, or get one cleaned, and maybe buy a pair of pants. The railroad's not a bad life though. But university might do me good. What would I take? Engineering? Jim says I should study English and finish my Diary Book. That might be okay too, you know. Fifteen years old. You'd never guess. And sitting in the bar like that. And drinking too. Or was she? And what a snapper, Ray would say. It was I guess. Hairy. (I feel myself.) I sure hope Grandad's better now. I'd sure like working here with him. Be great to sit inside the cab and watch him drive. He doesn't like the diesels though. I hope he's going to be okay. Dad said all right.

James Edward Puddle. What a goddamn name. GADDAMN, he says. I hope there's no damn cops around. Be great to land in jail right now. JESUS. She wouldn't call the cops, she wouldn't dare. Shit she was fucking Ray Malone. I wonder how she was in bed. Big bitch boy! Old Ray can pick them up okay. Frog-stickin, he calls it. Crazy hell!

Quebec City was a crazy weekend. Ray and me. He got one there and one for me. I can't even think of her goddamn name. Thérèse. Marie. Or some damn thing. You have to talk French to score like that. I should study French. I'll get my money Monday morning, put half in the bank, and buy a shirt and pair of pants, and take the rest of it with me. Maybe Jim'll be home tomorrow ... I'll borrow coupla bucks till then. Hey listen to that bastard snore. James Edward Puddle damn ...

84// "NOW WHAT THE FUCK YOU DIRTY FUCK YOU GET YOUR FUCKIN HANDS OFF ME," and smash him in the ear and face and kick out in the goddamn dark and hear him whine and smash again a good one in the goddamn teeth. I cut my knuckles, kick again, and trip and fall.

He's running down the goddamn track. "YOU ROTTEN BASTARD, I'LL BREAK YOUR GODDAMN HEAD."

And scared again. The station cops will hear for sure. I lock the bunk car door and run.

85//   And back uptown. It's five o'clock. I'm tired too. I must have barely got to sleep. It's cold out now.

I walk along the street to Jim's. There's no car there. I walk around the back door way, up on the porch. And there's a big old hammock swing to flop down cold on, later waking up all stiff and sore. The sun is up, it's warmer now. I walk around the house again. No car here yet. It's Sunday and the store is closed. He could be out at Shediac. Too cold to swim, but nice inside the cottage now. So walk down town.

The night clerk in the station held my bag for me so pick it up and sneak it in the washroom there. I sure look greasy. Sunday too. So scrub myself with station soap (the green stuff, scented up with pine) and comb my hair. My shirt is wrinkled and my pants are too. Take off my shoes and wash my stinking railroad feet. Pack up my bag and leave it with the clerk again.

"I'll pick it up tonight for sure."

"Okay. We're not supposed to keep them here."

Then back outside I walk toward the road to Shediac. Hitch-hike and get there. Eight o'clock. Then walk along the sand road to the beach. And there's the cottage. No damn car. And boarded up. I'm hungry too. Those friends of Jim's! They have a cottage somewhere here. So walk some more.

Then back in Moncton, hitchhiked again, and sitting in the station there. Should borrow money from the clerk, he knows I'm working, but don't like to ask. I wish to hell that Jim was here. And then it's dark outside again. I'm starving now. And back outside. There's no one home at Jim's again so curl up in the hammock swing and try to sleep.

It's Sunday night, the gangs are back! I'll walk back to the station yard and look around.

"Signal Gang?"

"Yeah, Dan Dewar's."

"I think they're all out in the Hump Yard."

"How far is that."

"Oh, five, six miles."

"Which way?"

"Straight out there": pointing. "But you're not going to walk it are you."

"No, no, just asking."

"Okay, cause it's a long hike."

86// And walking out along the ties and counting them to take my mind off food and hoping Sammy might be there or anyone that I might know and counting ties and walking fast and walking slow and counting ties. And hours later see the lights.

87// And standing in the shadows of the cars out there,

and hearing voices talking, laughing, shouting, cursing. Sammy's car's not here goddamn. Too scared to knock or walk inside. But scared of what? Standing in the shadows of a half a dozen cars, that's me. Me'n my jeans and dirty shirt. I gotta borrow a buck or two. These men don't know me. Who are they? They're railroadmen. And just can't bring myself to knock. What's wrong with me? And walking back along the track my throat is aching with a lump and sitting down at last it breaks. I'm on the track and crying, sobbing, to myself. But no damn tears. I'm dry-eyed sobbing, choking on a lump inside my throat and it's dry too. O JESUS CHRIST, I'm cold and hungry and I should be home. O JESUS CHRIST.

It's midnight when I'm back on Jim's swing and sleep at last.

88// Monday and it gets hot again. And I'm awake at six to walk down town. There's no one in the station yet so out on empty gut and aching legs I walk again, down streets I've never walked before, but all around the station part of town. Some people on the way to work and into diners with steamed up windows and the smell of bacon and coffee, and what I wouldn't give right now for a glass of milk. Just walking walking walking walking, ending at the station once again. Six forty-five. Then stop awhile, rest my feet, and walk again.

And look at me: old beat-up shoes, same dirty shirt, and old blue jeans, my face is clean (I washed up in the can again) but feels damn dirty anyway. All tired now with aching legs and empty gut.

And walk some more …

89// Old station clock:

7:05

7:08

7:12

7:17

7:21.

90// And walk again …

91// It's eight o'clock!

I'm up those stairs and opening that office door, not hungry now, but feeling good, and looking in for anyone, and there's the guy said engineers come from the ranks, and two more guys just standing there, and wow, a pretty girl beside a desk. She looks at me.

"Pete -------, Eddie Linden's gang in Rivière Bleu. I have to pick my cheque up now my Grandad's sick. I'm going home …"

"I'm sorry": smiles at me.

And slowing down to say again what I've just said.

"Oh cheques! ... Don O'Brien handles those. He comes in at nine ...."

92//   So back inside the station now:

8:12

8:15

8:17.

GODDAMN THAT CLOCK and back outside.

93//   "Don O'Brien?"

"Yessir."

"Peter --- ... I'm with Eddie Linden's gang in Rivière Bleu ... my Grandad had a stroke and I got called home ... I thought I could pick up my cheque before it went out to the gang ...."

"Linden's gang?"

"Yessir."

"Those cheques went out Friday."

JESUS CHRIST.

(But thinking fast): "Dan Dewar's gang, where's it at now?"

"Dewar ... Dewar ... That's in Amherst now."

(My old friend Sam!): "Thank you, Thank you." (And

thinking again): "Can I wire the gang from here and have my cheque sent back?"

"Sure."

"I got no money ..."

"I'll send it for you."

"When do you figure it would get here?"

"Oh ... Friday, at the latest ..."

Thank you, thank you: and out again and scanning sche¬dules on the station board and there it is: AMHERST 10:45 AM DAILY. Not hungry now but planning everything I have to do. I get my bag from the station clerk and hit the washroom once again and scrub up quick, then sit down waiting for the train.

Then on the train.

And on the way.

And in the Amherst Station, starving now.

94// "SAMMM!"

"JESUS CHRIST!"

I start to cry, I don't know why, but laugh and cry all over Sam, and try to tell him best I can how goddamn hungry scared I am.

"It's okay, boy ..."

"No, Jesus, Sam": and look at him, big pretty man. I'm

okay now. And cry again. I blurt it out, the Rivière Bleu and old Mama, the cops, and broke, and Jimmy gone.

"It's okay, boy …"

But cry some more. "I never shoulda left here Sam. It's all gone wrong." And tell him of the telegram and dig it out for him to read. And Sammy puts his arm round me … It's okay boy.

95// And Oh, the smell of frying eggs and frying ham. And Sam working at the stove and telling me to sit back down, and serving me. Orange juice, toast, big mug of milk, and eggs and ham, more milk, and finally a big hot cup of railroad tea, and talk with Sam. It's almost noon. I tell Sam how I think I'll go to university. I'll save my cheques from here on in. My Mom and Dad want me to go. I like the railroad, really Sam, but one more year should do me though.

And Sam lends me thirty bucks and tells me to wash up in the cars and then get started straightaway for home. "You go on home. They'll hold your cheque. You go home first. And DON'T let no one see you here. You get the train at 5:05. Stay out of sight. And let me know how Billy is" (Grandad). "You send that money when you get your cheque."

96// MEMORY VI: Amherst, Nova Scotia, July: A workgang on the siding down the track lights up. It's after suppertime. The houses, flatback to the track, stare out at you. Old clotheslines hanging to the trackbed's edge, sag heavy grey with washing from the floors above. Five stories up on the trackside is two above the street out front. Two floors half buried in the bank along the track. It's here you saw the children play the games of dare. You're sitting on a reefer top to cool off in the early night. You watch and hear the whispers and the dares. Five Coke bottles will buy a chocolate bar, but fifty cents will buy enough for all. Five faces daring up at you:

—You got money?

—No.

—You got fifty cent?

—No.

—FUCK OFF: and four young boys and one young girl run laughing in between the cars. Just up the track, the glow of lamps, the workgang cars, say try again. The whispers all but reach your ears. Two rocks are tossed against a door.

—You got bottles?

—Nope.

—You got money?

—Yeah.

—You got twenty-five cent?

—Yeah.

Then whispering, excited now. The time has come. The street lights on the bank above come on.

—You got fifty cent?

—Yeah.

Then whispering again. —You got fifty cent?

—Yeah. Yeah.

Two oldest of the five step out, and to the ladder from the door. They whisper here, then join the others, whispering again. The man steps back inside the car. The lamp goes out. The little girl is helped up through the door and four young boys sit back to wait ...

The games of the poor.

97// Now back in Amherst for a loan from Sam and walking down those streets again, and thinking things like that and more, and all around the station part of town. My train goes out at 5:05, so have the afternoon to kill; not hungry now, but feeling good and thinking back to Ray Malone and wondering if he's okay. People on verandahs watch me pass, and watch me closer when I pass again. I change my route and walk some more. I buy myself a shirt to wear and put it on in the station washroom. Throw the other one away. I'm feeling good and think about a quart of beer, got money now, and thirsty too so what the hell and up the street to a liquor store and back toward the track with one. And feeling big as hell again.

Got money now and on the train at 5:05 and just like payday feeling good, and wishing Ray Malone was here to get more beer and have a time. Then think of Grandad and getting home tomorrow sure.

98// I remember one payday, which like all the others, began with seven minutes at a writing pad to see you're getting all your overtime, ran on through a break-your-back, without-a-waterboy day, maybe a mile from the nearest spring, and ended in a small hotel. Ray Malone and I working as a nut gang back the track behind the crew (a welcome break from swinging pick), and laughing in the morning sun. We spend the day together, drifting one, two miles behind the gang and double checking nuts and bolts at signal, relay box, or switch, along the track. And sometimes catching up again:

"WE HERE TO CHECK YO NUTS": Ray'd grin at the gang in his finest imitation of some Halifax sailor, waving his socket wrench menacingly at one or two of the men. Then catching breath while they worked on ahead again. Day's like that I was happy's hell and stumbled along the tar hot ties, scuffing my boots in the limestone trackbed.

On this particular payday, Ray made up one of his many songs. And this particular song he liked so well that he carried it with him from the New Brunswick border right on to wonderful old Quebec City, where he sang it one day sitting on the track to a little bunch of school kids going home to supper, study, sleep. The song he sang to them, if I can remember a bit of it, went something close to:

> Gonna fine me a wooman
> somewhere'n this lan,
> big fat wooman,
> to hole my han ....
> When I'm awaaay,
> my woman gonna say ....
> Oh I married to a raileroaderman,
> Oh I married to a raileroaderman.

Just little kids, six, seven years old and standing at the trackside, their big black brown eyes shining like dogs' eyes and smiling really weird smiles at Ray and not one of them under¬standing a goddamn word he was singing.

But off they ran anyway, laughing and shouting in French, except one little fella running knock-kneed, book-bag bouncing on his ass, who kept yelling, "RAILROADMAN RAIL ROAD MAN RAIL ROAD MAN" until we couldn't see him anymore.

"Mama! Papa! … *J'ai vu un vagabond!*"

99// Hopping freights, motorcars, passengers, or in cars Ray borrowed from a good-head guy, you'd head for villages come to you by whispered word from up the track. Riding cold in a boxcar, toolcar, sometimes on a flatcar, fifty miles in your loafers, jeans, and open-neck white shirt. Sitting crazily crowded on those yellow and black, sit-em-on-the-track, work gang motorcars (manufactured by some company the name of which has disappeared). Drinking forty, fifty miles on a padded passenger making its way from Halifax or Moncton on into Montreal (or maybe even right across Canada) with your pass, and catching conversations with your hungry ears that never seemed to get accustomed to the FUCK ME, FUCK YOU banter of the many-miled work gang. Reeling drunkenly along some never-seen-before dirt road through backwoods Quebec, with nothing to go on but things like ONCE YOU PASS THE ELEVENTH BRIDGE TURN LEFT, and maybe four quarts of warm beer.

100// Ah! That was fun!

101// And times when all the fun of it began to fade. Night after night and all day long with men who'd lost the railroad from their bones. The talk is not the railroad talk of Grandad's day, the sound of trains, the smell of coal and engine smoke, the whistle in the night-time dark. Along the track and ditches of the day, and at the heaping tables in the cars, God, even in the bunks at night, it's dirt.

This woman in some little town who's screwing school boys just to keep away the pain of growing old. Some high school girl in some small town who's clapped up one whole hockey team. Some wife in neighbourhoods where you've not been. Some whore in someone's own hometown. Some bitch. Some tail. Some Screw. Some Cunt. SOME DIRTY STINKING FUCK ALONG THE TRACK.

Was all that fun?

102// And feeling so, arrive in Moncton at seven-thirty that Monday night September 4, 1959; get drink, drank, and got drunk, took a room in a side-street hotel, a room with a back-yard-sized sagging bed, and fell asleep, waking up the next morning with $14.41 and don't know why, but out again and to a liquor store.

Poor Grandad. Poor old me. And poor old railroad. Every damn thing's changed today. The whole dream's gone. I don't know why.

I showed the desk my union card and told the clerk about my cheque. He says they don't give credit, so I pay $9.00 (up to Friday morning). Three bucks a night, No meals.

Then go upstairs and write another letter home. It's noon and so I walk up town, and walk into the Record Room. But Jim's not back and some strange girl says Jimmy and his Mother and his Father are on holidays and can she help me? When will he be back? In two weeks.

And Friday gets here, finally. I get my cheque. And get my bag from station clerk, and take the whole load back to the hotel. I pick out shirts and pants and things and send it all out to get cleaned. I cash my cheque and buy another night in that big bed. And then a meal in the dining room and a two-buck tip.

103//
Rivière Bleu, Que.
September 8, 1959

Dear Mom and Dad:

The fellow going to take my place arrives here today, I am told. They seem to be in an awful hurry to get this job done. But the way things look today, I will be able to leave tonight or tomorrow morning. I hope Grandad is well. And Grandma too.

Am very anxious to get home and see him and see all of you.

Love to everyone,
Peter

104// It's Friday night: "You ever have TWO girls in bed?" The desk clerk calling me aside.

I tell him no.

"Have you got any booze in your room?"

I tell him no.

He whispers to me: "If you had a couple of bottles of gin in your room, I know a couple of girls who have been dying to meet you ..."

105// It's nine o'clock and here's the gin, delivered here by cab, of course, and there I sit, all nervous now, and in my head all sorts of crazy wild things to come. I've never tasted gin before. And JESUS CHRIST, if Ray was here! I sit and wait. And sit and wait and drink. And sit and wait and drink some more. And tap tap tap against my door. I open it and there they are.

PART 5

106// A great big bed with cranked-up head and bent knee-rest all draped in coarse white sheet and feather puff with pillows all around the place, and water, ginger ale, and pills, and cards and flowers and sadness and chairs for those who come to sit; it's in the living room. Grandad is home. And here I am just sitting there not knowing what in hell to say.

107// "Where were you?"

"You got my letters, didn't you?"

"Peter it's been about a goddamn month!"

"What's today?"

"The sixteenth!"

"Look, I told you in my letters, Dad, we just can't up and take off any time we want to. It's a big job. An important job.

They couldn't let me go until they arranged for someone to come in and fill for me."

"Where were you?"

"In Rivière Bleu, for crisakes!"

"Your letters were postmarked Moncton?"

"I explained that. NOW FOR THE LAST TIME when you mail letters from any road gang they go through Moncton."

"Your letters from Nova Scotia weren't postmarked Moncton."

"IN QUEBEC THEY WERE. NOW DO YOU BELIEVE ME?"

"I phoned Moncton last Wednesday. They said you hadn't been in Rivière Bleu for three weeks."

"We weren't right in Rivière Bleu, we were thirty miles up the track."

"How come head office didn't know that?"

"How the hell should I know."

"It strikes me funny."

"It strikes me funny too."

"Don't they keep track of their gangs?"

"I DON'T KNOW … they probably just looked at a map and didn't see my name in Rivière Bleu. I was thirty miles up the damn track." (For Christ sake.)

"They said the gang was there but you weren't."

"I KNOW THAT, I KNOW THAT. The MAIN gang was in Rivière Bleu but Ray Malone and myself and two other guys were on a checking crew. THIRTY MILES UP THE TRACK."

"They said they hadn't seen Ray Malone in three weeks either."

"LOOK, I don't know how they screwed it up. But they did. We were thirty miles up the track. They didn't know it. JESUS CHRIST!"

"They said you were through."

"Through?"

"Fired."

"Oh come off it. Come off it. Come off it, will you."

108// My Grandad lying there and all doped up. His head is up. His knees are up. He stares into his collar bone. And neighbours keep on dropping in to sit in kitchen chairs and stare at him and talk at Grandma in the kitchen or the hall and tell her of a thousand relatives who have had strokes far worse than Grandad's. (And today they are all walking around as though nothing had happened to them.) Some bring cakes and pies, and some of them bring bread and rolls, and some of them bring cookies and squares. They don't know what to bring Grandad.

I wish I could bring him the railroad. A fireman. Or take him out of bed and to the roundhouse.

Poor Grandma, running all around the house and trying to find things to keep her busy, can't find anything.

She would like to bake, but we have seven pies, four cakes, and large tin cans of cookies and squares. And nine loaves of bread. She'd like to clean the house up, but Mom and Mrs. Payne from next door have done that. Maybe she'd even like to be alone. Or cry. I don't know. But she can't do that. People keep telling her funny stories about things Grandad used to do. She can't remember any of this. She's left with nothing left to do, and too too many people in the house to pray.

Once she went into her bedroom and was kneeling by her bed with her beads and someone went to look for her and found her and thought she had fallen down so called everyone in the house into the bedroom to pick her up and put her on the bed. This made me cry and made her happy because then she could look after me. But then my Mother came in and told me to stop bothering my poor Grandmother.

I sit by Grandad in the living room. He's sleeping. I bet he's dreaming trains again. His big red face is yellow now. He looks like he's lost fifty pounds. I wish he'd wake up and tell me a story. I wish he'd wake up and see me here.

They don't tell stories like you used to do. I guess there's nothing left to tell. He lies there. His head is tipped up so he can breathe, and he just wheezes. His big jug ears look awful dry. And so's his hair. He needs a shave. The house is almost empty now. It's suppertime and sister Kate is back home now. It's after school and she gets work to do. And Grandma's in her bedroom now.

109// It's quiet in this house tonight, and no one talks. My Dad is reading in the dining room while Mom and Kate clean up the after-supper mess. And Grandma sits beside Grandad, alone at last. A freight train shakes the house, but doesn't blow for the crossing at our front door. The Brotherhood of Railroad Engineers. I sit by Grandma for a while, and then to bed.

> **110//** MEMORY VII: Now no one cares. The kids don't care. The railroad ends at five o'clock. It's like a goddamn grocery store and no one takes it home at night. The railroad's gone. It's not the same.

111// I open up the window in my room to watch a diesel just come into town without a sound. I hear my Grandma go to bed and wipe my eyes, then to sleep.

> **112//** He died that night and was buried three days later in the Catholic cemetery in the other end of town, a good eight miles

from the nearest railroad track. His pall-bearers were two engineers and four firemen from the local brotherhood. And there were flowers in your house and at his graveside from railroad families all over town. And railroadmen and wives called around to see your Grandma, the wives hugging her and crying, the men staring awkwardly at the shiny toes of their boots sticking out of the legs of their trousers and thinking back to other engineers who had gone before. And there was a wreath from the President of the National Railways who had personally sent Grandad a letter to go with his twenty-five-year watch about twenty years ago, and later in the week there was a letter from Montreal outlining how your Grandad's pension would be paid to his widow in equal monthly instalments. And somebody at the funeral said something about That Big Roundhouse in the Sky and somebody else said how nice it was that you were on the railroad, the same way he had been, and your Grandma cried through her veil and your mother cried because it was her father, and your sister

cried to see her mother crying, and you and
your father stood tight-lipped through it all,
determined to look like men, and everything
went like clock-work except for the quick
looks the priest got when he accidentally
threw a stone with his little handful of gravel
at the casket, and everyone looked sad, and
said it was the nicest funeral they had ever
attended, and then they left the graveyard,
and they went home.

WATCHA GONNA DO BOY ... WATCHA GONNA
BE? You ask yourself.

113//   Moncton, N.B.
                            September 23, 1959

Dear Mom and Dad:

I don't quite know how to begin this, but I have to write it.
You were right. I went back to the station as soon as I arrived
here and was told that I am fired. I should have believed you.
I would have saved myself a trip down here for nothing.

I don't know what to say about the letters. I only wanted
to please you as I always try to. I guess it is time I stopped
kidding myself and decided to behave more like a young
man should. Perhaps if I had been doing this I wouldn't be

in this mess today. You were also right about the money. If I had taken out a Canada Savings Bond when you told me to I could still have enough to get me started on my first year of university today. I do have about $100 saved, and there is no reason for you to do this, but if you would even lend me the money I would be able to pay you back next summer. I was talking to someone here today, and they said that special arrangements could be made to register even this late. If you still want me to go and will lend me the money I will. The only alternative will be to find another job and work the full year as we had originally planned.

I did like the railroad, and if there was any chance of my becoming an engineer, I would do it in a minute. Please tell Grandma that. But today, even to be an engineer, they want you to have some university.

I know I should have gone right home when you wired me. But when I got to Moncton I ran into a bunch of old friends and got carried away. What started out as a good idea fell apart. I will be home tomorrow as soon as I can collect all my old things together and we can decide what I'm going to do then.

I hope you can forgive me. I know I don't deserve it. But I am very very sorry.

Love, your son,
Peter

I wrote that letter on the train and put it in my pocket with the rest. Then sat embarrassed by myself and thought about the morning and my Dad. He walked me to the station in the rain. He said to call, or let him call. He said it didn't matter; not to go. "You're not the first boy fired from a job! It's not a crime!" But off I go.

He gave me this big envelope and left. I climbed on board and took a seat.

"Here, read this": that's what he said to me. "It's not very funny but it's about the railroad. I think there's a moral in it too."

The train is moving when I pick it up. I rip it open and it spills: My letters! Every goddamn one!

And pick them up and sit back sick, embarrassed, by myself, and think. OF ALL THE DIRTY GODDAMN TRICKS. Of all the dirty tricks to pull. My Grandad dies. I'm feeling bad enough right now. And he does this. And sit there cursing as the train roars on. OF ALL THE DIRTY GODDAMN TRICKS. And curse him fifty miles or more.

114// The train is full of fat and happy people and scowling me, mad at Dad, mad at the railroad, mad at the world (boxed in my own damn lies with no back door). O Grandad in heaven, what in hell will I do now? If I still have a job, I'll never go home again.

Through Bathurst (home of big blonde cheerleader girlfriend of high school days), and across the brown backwoods of New Brunswick for miles and miles in the rain. Here houses built from packing crates and patched with Coca-Cola signs, where many a thirsty tourist stops: "Canteen? CANTEEN? Why hell this here's my house!"

115// And boyhood memory: "YOU CAN'T SWIM THERE, IT'S FULLA SHIT."

"O YEAH!"

116// And so to Moncton where the sun is out. And to the Record Room and Jim is back all full of laughs and holidays and tell him how my Grandad died and use his phone:

"Ah, I'm calling for a Peter ------, ah, he asked me to call for him. He's ah still at home his Grandfather died you know and he, ah, was wondering where his gang is now he'll probably be going back to work Monday."

Then playing records in the Record Room and eating in Marcil's across the street; clean restaurant full of sexy French Catholic working girls from offices next door and upstairs. Late afternoon I walk downtown and in the station yard turn in my pass (to a station cop): "I, ah, found this on the train this afternoon. I wonder if you could turn it in to whoever looks after them?"

And walking out again and JESUS CHRIST! It's RAY MALONE! "HEYYY, PETEY BOY!"

Ray just got in here yesterday. He's going home. I tell him how my Grandad died, and how I just got canned today. He says she never called the cops but sent two big bastard brothers of hers around to look for me, and when they went back and told her I was gone, she told them it was Ray Malone!

"The goddamn frog": he grabs me by the arm and off we go. He says he took off in a big hurry but just fixed it up with head office, and now he's taking two weeks holidays until the gang moves further up the track. "HEY, HEYYY, IT'S GOOD TO SEE YOU THOUGH!"

And here's Big Ray and me again, and watching him walk farm-like down the street, sometimes ahead of me and talking back, and always grabbing me in hugs, and laughing now at me and Rivière Bleu:

"The FUNNIEST THING I EVER SAW BARE ARSE AND JUMPING OUT THE DOOR LIKE THAT. O PETEY, if you coulda seen yourself you woulda laughed like hell. HAAAAAAAA. O PETEY BOY, HAAAAAAAA. BARE DAMN ASS."

And here's another Ray Malone. He's off the track and

all dressed up and saying things like WELL NOW THERE to girls along the street and making conversation with a passer-by. His old tweed coat and polka-dot tie make him a gentleman. We stop in a restaurant where he combs his hair in the mirror in the Coke machine and buys two Coke; for us. We sit. He slaps his leg and punches me: "HEYYYYY, PETEY BOY!" The waitress smiles, then laughs at him. "WELL NOW THERE, what are you doing tonight … ?" And people in the place all turn to look.

And back out on the street again "I got a friend in the Legion here can sign us in." And: "Where'n hell you stayin tonight?"

"Hell, I don't know."

"Well stick around HEY PETEY BOY!" And whispering: "We just might do a little frog-stickin, eh?" And punching me again.

117// I phone Jim from the Legion Hall and tell him to join us after work. He's dying to meet my Ray Malone. I sit back down to drink with Ray and strange men at the table now. He introduces me. They're railroadmen. I drink and watch him talking now. Excited now, and sad, then smiling, laughing, nodding, whisper in an ear, and punch. His big feet planted flat against the floor and leaning out across the table to his friend.

"SIX BIG ONES," lemmee pay, I say.

"OKAY" says Ray. "OLD PETEY HERE. He works with me in Rivière Bleu," he's telling them. Then winking at me, laughing loud.

And one of the men here knew Grandad and I tell how he died and he says it's a goddamn crime the way all the best engineers are dying, and how goddamn small the pensions are. And another fellow there says all the best engineers are dead and how the new guys driving the new diesels are just a goddamn bunch of college punks. And another fellow there says the railroad's going all to hell. And pretty soon they're telling stories just like Grandad used to tell and talking about the old steam engines and how the goddamn railroad's getting rid of firemen with twenty years' seniority and the goddamn union isn't worth a damn. And Ray keeps butting in to say the only good men alive are railroadmen but how all the old ones are either retiring or dying and how there's too damn many young punks joining the railroad today who think they know everything and how they don't know sweet fuck all. I sit there spellbound.

Here's my railroad. Here's my goddamn railroad now. It's not dead after all. And I tell a couple of stories I heard from Grandad and everyone says they're good stories. And we sit and drink and talk like this for hours and hours.

Then Jim arrives (the doorman comes to ask for me) and one of Ray's friends signs him in. I introduce him, first to

Ray Malone and they shake hands, then Ray rhymes off the names around the table, and Jim all dressed to kill is sober from working all day.

Here's Ray: "Petey has told me so much about you, Jim, that I feel like I been sleeping with you. AAAAAAAA." And everybody at the table laughs. And Jim has a couple of beers with us and it's six o'clock. It's suppertime in the railroad world and Ray's friends have to go to eat. "WHAT SAY WE ALL COME BACK TONIGHT AND BRING SOME GIRLS": that's Ray again. And everybody says that's great, to meet them here at nine o'clock. And Jim says meet him at Marcil's, he's got to go home to eat now too.

118// THE CROWN HOTEL: "That's it! That's it!" I'm telling Ray. "My whole damn pay cheque. Two of them. They ate with me. They slept with me. Just drunk as Jesus every day. I never had so damn much fun. That's it! That's it!"

And leaning at the desk clerk now: "You ever have two girls in bed?"

He looks at me.

"You ever have two girls in bed?"

He turns away.

"Aw c'mon buddy, this's my old friend Ray Malone. He's okay. C'mon, c'mon. Where are they, eh?"

"I'm sorry," he says, "do I know you?"

"DOES HE KNOW ME. JESUS, RAY. GET HIM. GET HIM. DO I KNOW YOU? DOES HE KNOW ME? JESUS CHRIST!"

But get a room there anyway when Ray smooth-talks the clerk a bit, and now upstairs. (A different room with two big beds.)

And telling Ray: "The dirty bugger, Ray. The two of them. It cost me more'n a hundred bucks. Big redhead and that dirty blonde. I'll eat it off, she kept saying. I'll eat it off." And Ray's got his gear from the station now. His banjo and his overnight.

"O JESUS, RAY": me rolling on the bed. I'm drunk: "O JESUS, RAY." And demonstrating: "I was on top like this and the other one kept doing this. Look Ray, this, like this. AAAAA HAAAAA. It cost me more'n a hundred bucks. They stayed Friday night and Saturday and Sunday and Monday and Tuesday and Wednesday and Thursday and I didn't get home until Saturday morning. O JESUS, RAY, ooooooeee!" And Ray laughs too.

119// And eight o'clock it's just like back in Rivière Bleu; Ray hogging up the sink so bad I have to wait until he gets through. This madman washing is a sight to see with water flying everywhere around the bathroom, dropping soap and spitting in the toilet bowl. His lips curl back and he inspects his yellow teeth. He smacks his lips and has to wipe the mirror off. His hairy shoulders rounded from the track work and splashing like an elephant with aftershave.

"That saves a lotta washin, yesiree!"

Lavoris rumbles in his throat, runs down his chin. He rubs it in his hairy chest and spits the rest out in the bowl. He runs his fingers through his hair, Lavoris, soap, and water slick it down. He smiles at me: "You ready yet?"

"I'd drown around that goddamn sink!"

"C'mon. C'mon."

Then washing up, I see him hauling on his tie, a blue with polka dots he found somewhere. He jerks it tight and grins in the mirror over my head.

"I'm sumpthin ain't I really though?"

"You sure's hell are!"

120// I telephone Jim and tell him where I am and when I'll meet him at Marcil's. And Ray and I go downstairs for a bite to eat.

"Just look at that bastard standing there": that's me to Ray: "Do I know you? And Christ he got the gin for me." And Ray says not to worry none, he's got his job to think about. And I say I suppose that's true.

The fresh air picks me up a bit and walking off toward Marcil's, I clear my head.

121// MEMORY VIII: Forgetting everything about the railroad in the cool fall air and thinking only of the night ahead. Tomorrow you go home again to patch things up and take another stab at life. Gone now the railroad dreams of little boyhood; memories of track and train and engineer and little you. Of brakemen with a heavy tired arm at end of day. When one man moved a track and moved a train.

The brakeman's out and fumbles for his key. The lock's undone, the handle on the switch is up, then slide and click. Direction changed. The leaning there until the tail goes by and slide and click the mainline's back. Or sitting in a warm caboose ... rrrroarrrrrrr, kuchunk kuchunk kuchunk kuchunk ... the engine and the cars gone by. Caboose door flapping in the wind at times, then caught and slammed. The brakeman's on the track again. How many times the slide and click of well-greased points? How many times the slammm of steel in steel where nimble fingers drop a pin to make a train? How many times that slipless jump from trackbed to a ladder rung and down again?

Of firemen inside the cab with fire burning on their necks and smell of steam and coal dust in the air. To bend with shovel in a black coal pile and throw black power in a roaring fire. To hear the engineer yell FIRE and shovel with your railroad guts and feel the sweat and coal dust mix across your back. How much power in a shovel of coal? Then sitting back and laughing in the wind on a downhill grade. A window all your own.

Forgetting you sprawled on the floor beside the stove, trying to study, with nothing on your mind but trains. Your mind made up at the age of four and steeped in railroad time and railroad talk, that you would be an engineer. And nowhere, never, did you change your mind.

Forgetting Janice Cassidy and a letter sent, which said you'd made your mind up now. (People like your father, Janice, and Harold Hay, have given me just what I needed. They've put the railroad back where it belongs. Inside. The railroad's gotta be a part of you!) And: (See you soon!).

This railroad sure ain't what it used to be!

122// I'M FIRED. I DIDN'T KNOW THAT THEN. IT'S DIFFERENT NOW!

And Jim is waiting at Marcil's and says he's got a date for me. And drink a milk shake. Talk a bit. And watch young couples strolling in.

When I told Jim about my getting back to Moncton with nowhere to go he said I should have gone to the big Cathedral across from the Record Room. Catholic Churches don't lock their doors, he said. You're allowed to go in and sit. He says it's too bad I got fired from the railroad, because now I'll never get to write my railroad book. But then we start to laugh again, just like always, talking foolish and kidding the waitress. Jim's like that: serious as a parent for a while, then madcap crazy like Ray and me; grinning at me through his green glasses and feeding dimes into the jukebox. Let's go, he says. We have to pick the girls up now, and out we go.

123// Claudette Leblanc wasn't a friend of Jim's at all. He had some friend of his call her up and make the date for me, and all night long she keeps asking me if I've known Walter long.

"Oh yeah. Oh yeah."

124// There's Ray Malone and a table load of railroad-men with wives. All drinking big green quarts of Moosehead. And one of Ray's friends signs us in and in we go and sit with them. Big Friday night at the Legion Hall. Jim with his beautiful girlfriend Bonnie with her shy brown eyes; me and Claudette, who is dressed to kill in a silky dress with a tight tight belt, and no damn sleeves. (I had my old grey sports coat on, and brown pants I'd bought in a general store in St. Eleuthère, Quebec.) And pretty soon everybody knows our names and Claudette is asking everyone if they have known Walter long. The railroad wives don't even look at her. But Ray Malone is winking at me and rolling his eyes back in his head, and it's warm in here and pretty soon I'm feeling good again.

Big railroadmen and two of them in railroad vests, all wearing black or dark blue shiny suits, with very mothery looking wives (as old as my own mother 250 miles away) and I don't even drink at home. It's Friday Night in the Legion Hall. It's good to be with Ray and Jim again.

LADIES AND GENTLEMEN, WELCOME TO OUR REGULAR FRIDAY NIGHT PARTY, AND A VERY SPECIAL WELCOME TO ANYBODY WITH US THIS EVENING FROM OUT OF TOWN. THE BAND IS READY ... SO LET'S DANCE! (And two, three couples go onto the floor.) AND REMEMBER, JUST BECAUSE IT'S DANCE TIME, YOU DON'T HAVE TO STOP DRINKING. HA HA HA ...

And it's just like back in Rivière Bleu, Ray watching me, and laughing loud. He's talking to a railroad wife with pudgy arms and big glass beads around her neck. She's laughing just as hard as he, and poking him in the side with her big round elbow POW, like OOW GOWAN! There's Jim and Bonnie dancing now. He winks at me and I wink back, and make a dirty sign at him. You can hear Ray laughing and talking right out here on the dance floor. Claudette is exactly my height, five foot eight in her high heels. The music stops. And someone buys a round of beer.

"What university do you go at?" She asks me that. Jim fed Walter an awful line.

"Mount Allison," I look at her.

"O's not very far away?"

"Fifty miles."

"Do you come at Moncton often?"

"I will from now on": (oooo) and look straight into her big horn rims and wink at her. She leans across and sucks my ear and the railroad wives don't even look at her. I get a hard-on sitting there and fix it so it won't show through my pants.

"I'll be right back. Don't you dare move!" She winks at me.

"Frog-sticker": Ray Malone whispers in my ear, and here comes Jim. We all take pisses in the trough and stand around and laugh a while. The can is filled with everyone; some talking, some pissing, some just leaning around the urinals smoking. Ray says, poking Jim in the ribs, if SHE comes back to the hotel with you I want seconds! And Jim punches me and we laugh like hell.

Just women at the table when I get back; the railroad wives all talking sweetly to Jim's girl Bonnie, and old Claudette beating her hands to the music on the table top. She wants to dance, so up we go on the crowded floor.

But WALTZ TIME, LADIES AND GENTLEMEN, AND WE HAVE A VERY SPECIAL REQUEST FOR A VERY SPECIAL COUPLE WITH US HERE TONIGHT ... MR. AND MRS. RENE LEBLANC WHO ARE CELEBRATING THEIR TWENTY-NINTH WEDDING ANNIVERSARY ... LET'S HEAR IT FOR THEM NOW! (And the band plays a little bit of "Too Old to

Cut the Mustard" and everybody laughs and claps like hell.)

And everybody claps some more, and I ask Claudette if they are related to her, and she says she doesn't think so. And it's waltz time like the big man said, and Claudette just sticks to me and around and around the floor we go. I'm pretty high, half-flying now, and press my body into hers. She sucks my ear.

"How old are you Claudette?"

"I'll be twenty-three on the twenty-three of December."

"And not married yet?" I give her a little squeeze.

"I guess I cannot find the right man yet."

"Am I the right man, Claudette?" (Oh Jesus!) And she starts to eat my other ear.

"Maybe."

And Ray sees this. He's sticking out his own big tongue behind her back. And just like Rivière Bleu again (Oh God, if Jim could have been there), I'm flying now and making frequent trips to the bar, and to the can, and one of the railroadmen has got an okay for Ray to play his banjo. It's intermission and a singsong starts. Three or four songs that everybody knows, then Ray sings one that he made up:

Oh the brakeman and the fire man
the big old engineer,

are loafing on a west-bound freight
a hunnert miles from here;
the wives are all at home tonight,
the whistle and the clang.
It's time to play, the men's away,
HERE COMES THE SIGNAL GANG!

O the railroad is the life for me
It makes a damn fine wife ...
By midnight I'll be far away
a havin the time a me life!

And before we know it there's a hundred people around our table joining in songs they know, or clapping their hands to songs they never heard before. Claudette is hanging on to me, she's high now too. And all too soon the whole night is over and the band is playing "Good Night, Ladies" and the party ends.

YES IT IS GOOD NIGHT LADIES, AND I HOPE YOU'VE ALL HAD A WONDERFUL TIME, AND ON BEHALF OF THE BOYS IN THE BAND, I'D LIKE TO SAY THAT WE'VE ENJOYED IT AS MUCH AS WE HOPE YOU HAVE, AND WE'LL SEE YOU ALL HERE AGAIN NEXT WEEK AT THE SAME TIME ... GOOD NIGHT NOW!

Someone suggests we go for Chinese food and everybody says damn fine. So out of the Legion, pile into two cars, and off we go to the Golden Dragon. Claudette on my knee, or rather just about between my legs, and necking crazy now with the biggest, longest tongue I have ever seen. I'm dizzy when my eyes are closed, so stop a while.

She says she wants to go to the hotel and I squeeze her tit in my hand and we're all curled up and the old railroad wife in the front seat looks around just as I'm opening my eyes to keep from getting sick. And Ray, beside me in the back seat, laughs like hell.

125// And many jokes in the Chinese restaurant: "What the hell is one-ton soup?" And: "Mushroom soup, velly little meat, velly little vegetable, mush room for swish around you spoon." (That was Jim.) And egg lolls and leg rolls and chickee flied lice and CHICKEN BALLS? Claudette is sitting between Ray and me (her hand dug in between my legs) and saying she doesn't like Chinese food. And Jim starts asking: "Wassamalla you?" And the food finally comes. And I get sick.

126// So many nights in Rivière Bleu ... the same damn thing. Old Ray and I, in Rivière Bleu and many other towns throughout Quebec, drinking and singing and dancing in the small hotels. "GOD JESUS, Ray I'm getting drunk!"

"C'MON, C'MON." And out we go, heading for another hotel. Staggering stumble drunks, the two of us. I don't know why. And every time, almost every night, up it would come. And sometimes I would fall and Ray would yell: "YOU'RE WEARING IT!" And getting up. And hanging on to Ray who's laughing so goddamned hard, he's falling too. But Jesus I can't hold it down and up it comes again, so goddamn round, like one big lump, you'd never think your throat was huge enough. And again tonight, just sitting there after that crazy car ride from the Legion Hall; just sitting there and next thing I know everybody's looking at me, and I feel funny and hot all over, and I jump up from the table and throw up all over the goddamn floor.

I'm in the Chinese bathroom now; door locked, and on my knees. Vomiting. Weak and shaking all over. O Mother Father Jesus Christ Grandad in heaven what in hell is the matter with me. Old Sam and Janice Cassidy. Goddamn Quebec and Goddamn Rivière Bleu.

"Hey, you okay?"

"Who's that?"

"Jim. You okay?"

Unlock the door and let him in. "Hey! Wassamalla you … frow up all ovah my restlaunt. Wassamalla you?" And I have to laugh at Jim which makes me feel a little better.

"C'mon. I paid your bill. Bon and I are going home. C'mon, I'll give you a lift."

"Where's that big bitch?"

"She's gone on home. Come on. Come on."

127// It's one o'clock and cold outside. September night in Moncton, New Brunswick. Friday night (or Saarday now) and black out too. I'm drunk as I have ever been (or ever hope to be again).

September 23, 1959, Dear Mom and Dad: I show that letter to Bon and Jim. She says it's good, and Jim prophesies that everything will work out fine. And drive along the empty city streets; down Main Street, looking for the Crown Hotel. We drive past the Blue Circle and there it is. And lots of: "Jim old pal. Bon you don't know how much I think of this guy. I think he's the nicest guy in the world. I mean that Jim and you know it. I think you're the greatest too, Bon. Both of you. You're both the greatest."

One-thirty now. "Good night Pete."

"GOOD NIGHT."

"Good night."

"GOOD NIGHT."

And up the creaky plankwood stairs of the Crown Hotel,

moaning and grunting like my old Grandad; home from a midnight run.

And Ray Malone says all's fair in love and war, and be a nice guy and fuck off now Petey Boy. And Claudette giggles and pulls the sheets up around her neck and sucks his ear, and I click the light off and walk back outside.

128// There's tricks to hopping trains I still don't know. But then it didn't matter much. I didn't care. You're supposed to run along the side until you're going fast enough, then hand on ladder, spring and swing. Ray taught me that.

"YOU GET ON FIRST," he's telling me.

I try.

"NO SWING YOURSELF, like this," he's on. And jumps back off.

I try again.

"ONCE MORE," he yells, and up I go. The train is moving faster now. I'm laughing like hell; shouldn't be, but laughing at him running there.

"NOW, HEEERE I COME, WAHOOOOO," and there he is, beside me on a boxcar ladder.

And times when he would spot an open car. And, "THROW YOURSELF and WESTERN ROLL WAHOOOOOOOO!"

And over beer I'd talk to Ray. And over lunch, or over

something we were trying to lift. I talked so much that in about five days I got telling him the same damn things again. And even though he didn't answer much, I knew Ray didn't mind me going on like that. I told him first about Grandad, then home, or places I had been so far. I even told him about the railroad.

Eight hours a day, and sometimes ten, we'd work along the sun hot track. "AIN'T WORTH THE SWEAT," Ed Hill complained those last two hours of overtime. "AIN'T WORTH THE SWEAT, AIN'T WORTH THE TIME." Then payday'd come and Ed like all of us would yell: "I'D RATHER BE RICH THAN TIRED BUT I'M BOTH!"

Much later, late at night I mean, like Ray Malone, I learned to say, "O GOD, THE OVERTIME."

And rainy days we'd muck about, up to our goddamn knees in mud and old rubber boots. Big rubber boots, all bought same size, which me and all the little guys would lose. You step in mud and take a step, boot stays behind and one mud sock.

And sun hot days with flies that came in thirsty, fighting-for-a-soft-spot swarms. They bit, they hurt, they made you bleed.

But fuck, who needs him anyway?

129// And so to walking in the street. Around the block and in a steamed up greasy spoon to watch the night life in this town. Big baggy eyes and wino breath of skinny little men with fat girlfriends (and I half expect to see James Edward Puddle) and other fellows just as old as me. God knows why they aren't home yet. And every now and then a cop.

GO HOME. GO HOME, you tell yourself. Then out to find a place to sleep.

130// MEMORY IX: Oh, you were mad in love with railroad then, and used to hold your breath in an off-¬the-kitchen bedroom just to hear him wheezing and scudding up those creaky plankwood stairs. Back from a late run. Your Grandad.

You'd hear his lunch can hit the table, hear him toss his greasy cap at that restless rocking chair beside the window, and hear him yawn his ready-for-the-sack, wide yawn HO DE HO DE HUM, just like that.

You'd hold your breath and hear him hang his heavy denim coat behind the stove and then fall in his rocking chair on top of his cap where grunting, he'd unwind the laces from the cuffs of his overalls.

Then dropping off to sleep you'd hear the clink of buckles at his bib and heavy sighs of home-again gladness. Then sleeping see him sitting in the window of his speeding train, red-faced, with fire in his eyes.

Then wake again CALUMP CALUMP his heavy half-soled boots would hit the floor.

And sleep again as he began a midnight snack, alone in his own home.

Then you again, age seven, going to school, already in Grade II, standing at a crossing in the middle of town and reaching out with skinny nervous hands to touch the ladders on the boxcars creeping by. Bookbag in the dirt beside the track, and many times forgotten there, you'd spellbound wait to whop your hand against the outstretched leather glove of brakeman Billy Dean, or Joe Boudreau, who knew you as your Grandad's boy and watched for you.

The train gone by, you'd press your hand against the warm steel rail, then later, bookbag hanging from one shoulder, stop at Hamel's Corner Store where hung up just above the till was one big picture, three feet long, of one long train; and there you'd buy a b-b bat.

Back home at last and supper on, with Mom and Dad and Grandma, sister too, where halfway through the meal he'd set the plates to rattle on that kitchen table as he hauled a hundred people past his home. Five o'clock darkness in those late fall afternoons with five of us around the table hungry; slurping soup, or even stew (the way my Grandma made it).

Then times when he'd be home to eat; racing us to the bottoms of our bowls, he'd chomp and suck and blow upon his spoon, ruining your sister's supper, her with her weak stomach, and looking all the while to you like folk-song hero Casey Jones.

Big roly-poly wind-burned man with twinkling Merry-Christmas eyes, whose every bite would hiss and smack like appetite itself.

Sssslrrrp ... aaah ... ssLrrrp ... mmm.

Your after-suppers like the after-suppers of a thousand railroad families in a thousand railroad towns, spent in the kitchen to the sounds of dishes being washed, and crack of wood in the red-hot stove, and the creak of you-know-who beside the window in his rocking chair.

You share the house, the six of you, and don't talk much.

But picture you sprawled on the floor beside the stove, trying to study, with nothing on your mind but trains. Your mind made up at the age of four, and steeped in railroad time and railroad talk, that you would be an engineer.

131// And NOWHERE, NEVER, did I change my mind!

132// And I remember too those waking-up mornings when the bunk car smelled of ham and eggs, and stepping into dirt-stiff dungarees and yawning my breath against the morning air. Too late to shave, too late to wash, just splash your face and wipe it with a soggy towel.

Remember too, half numb with sleep, those dishes on the table, heaped with eggs that stared at you, a yolk-eyed, half-sick smile. And then the stinging morning sun squints up my eyes and sweats me so I smell myself.

It's two o'clock and I told Jim I'd be off home for sure

today, and when he sees me he'll ask me why. So wander off along the street. Thinking of Grandad working with Sam on the I.N.R., and laughing to myself, now cold. I dig for dimes, the coffee's hot, but just find two. I buy another coffee, back outside, and think of Mom and Dad and school; of school-day buddies now all gone. MY SON'S IN UNIVERSITY. WHERE'S YOURS? Aw, he's on the railroad I guess. And find in my hip pocket, all crumpled dead, that goddamn telegram: GRANDAD PARALYZED STOP STROKE STOP DOCTOR SAYS WILL NEVER WALK AGAIN STOP CAN YOU GET HOME? And thinking to myself, yeah, I'll be home. And fold it neat and stick it in my shirt for memory. Remember Sam? I bet he's warm in bed by now. Home for the weekend. I wonder who washes his dishes on Friday now? And Mom and Dad. MY SON'S IN UNIVERSITY. WHERE'S YOURS? Hell, I don't know. AND WATCHA GONNA DO BOY ... WATCHA GONNA BE?

133// This little old lady I see, standing by the corner of a huge stained glass, stone, and twenty-two-stepped Cathedral. Standing by the corner and just back out of sight between buttress and wall. I'm on the lawn. She's covered face and body with that make-you-wanna-travel railroad dirt and rubbing sweaty hands across her wind-burned forehead. Strikes me funny, so I'm laughing where I'm lying in the morning shade of a churchyard tree just off St.

George Street in Moncton. Just looks odd, that's all. There's women stepping out of cars driven by grey old men in pyjamas who are off and home again for Sunday morning rest. Hot Sunday Maritime sun for September. Chub-faced women in their forties and I am just a kid. Wrapped in their favourite colours. And every other car, a young couple. HE JUST DON'T TRUST HE ALONE, NO MATTER WHERE! And this little old lady! September, 1959, and here I am dreaming of Sam and Grandad and home, and thinking of God and prayers in Rivière Bleu. Fired in Moncton, not four days ago, and living in a greasy spoon, on moonlit lawns, and anybody's back-porch swing. That railroad sure ain't what it used to be.

END

AFTERWORD

Photo courtesy of Rekha Samuel

Peter Taylor was born in northern New Brunswick on Canada's east coast where, as he tells it, he was introduced to paper at a very early age – first by his father who was manager of the local pulp and paper mill, and later as a delivery boy for his hometown's weekly newspaper. Following high school, some stints on the railroad, and several years of university, Taylor signed on as a reporter with the Saint John *Telegraph-Journal*, then a leading daily in the province, and later spent close to ten years with *The Ottawa Citizen*, one of Canada's major news outlets. It was while with *The Citizen* that he began work on *Watcha Gonna Do Boy ... Watcha Gonna Be?*, a first novel which was subsequently made into a TV movie and later a radio drama by the Canadian Broadcasting Corporation (CBC).

Published originally by McClelland & Stewart, Canada's pre-eminent book publisher at the time, the novel in a roundabout way led to Peter joining that publishing house where within a very few years, he was named the company's Vice President and Marketing Director.

Watcha Gonna Do Boy ... Watcha Gonna Be? is a coming-of-age novel about a young man's dream of following in his grandfather's footsteps instead of heading off to university. He sees himself as the breakaway, the one who learns, not in the feedbag university, but in the streets, around the station part of town. It is also a book about discovery – the discovery of what it means to grow from the dreams of one's teenage years into the happy, reckless, and sometimes disturbing reality of young manhood. And it is filled with people from all sides of the tracks – pick-swinging Railroad Ray Malone and other members of a salty railroad gang, old women of the streets in rundown shoes, a wise-beyond-her-years fifteen-year-old girl, and always, over his shoulder, the shadow conscience of his railroad engineer and hero grandfather, his parents, and the hip sanity of his closest friend, Jimmy Solomon.

The New Brunswick of his teenage years, Taylor makes it clear, was quite removed from what came to be referred to as "the two solitudes" – French on the one side, English on the other. In his time, Taylor wrote in the biography of the first paperback edition, "French frogs were French frogs, and the rest of us were mostly Irish or Protestant bastards and we threw rocks at each other, called each other dirty names, and had a helluva lot of fun." Asked about it later, Taylor said that "there were tensions and separations, socially and economically, but for us, these played out day-to-day, face-to-face, in the streets and in the bars, the mills, labour yards, the dancehalls and hotel rooms. Here sprang a language — and often a swaggering attitude toward French Canadians, and French Canadian women in particular — things I witnessed as a kid and especially, during my early years working on the railway. And this I took to give gritty reality to the book."

In the recently launched *New Brunswick Literary Encyclopedia* (on-line from St. Thomas University in Fredericton at http://w3.stu.ca/stu/sites/nble/index.aspx), Elizabeth Harrison – St. Thomas graduate 2013 – describes *Watcha Gonna Do Boy...* as predating "the the work of Ray Fraser and David Adams Richards, and is thus monumental in pioneering a tone and subject matter that they would adopt a few years later."*

In Taylor's entry, another critic describes the novel as similar to the work of Jack Kerouac and others of the Beat Generation. Taylor even references the work of Kerouac in his novel: "For this is the year of Kerouac and the Beat Generation, and ... since the young men of America were getting so much praise about and for so many of the things we were doing ourselves right here in backwoods New Brunswick, we too would write books about it all."

David Helwig, in The *Tamarack Review*, says Taylor was indeed influenced by the music and literature around him, but more importantly suggests that he had the uncanny ability to create distinctly Canadian ways of discussing the restlessness within his own particular world.

"Times have changed and so have relations between French and English," says Taylor, "yet each generation we have seen since this book was published experienced the same restlessness and anxiety as Peter, the main character in the novel. Today, they just take different roads."

* One wonders what the critic for the *The Fredericton Gleaner* would think of Taylor's influence today. After the book was released in 1967 he wrote: "Some months ago I had occasion to make some caustic remarks about a book called *Beautiful Losers* [Leonard Cohen]. I found it nauseating, immoral and, in my opinion, pornographic. Now I hear that the same publisher has brought out an equally filthy book called *Watcha Gonna Do Boy ... Watcha Gonna Be?* My informant, a reliable book reviewer, tells me it is quite the filthiest book he has ever read."

3058

CPSIA information can be obtained at www.ICGtesting.com
Printed in the USA
LVOW06s2236230215

428028LV00003B/23/P

9 781554 553235